Alan Harrington is the author of eight books. Among these are *Life in the Crystal Palace* ('a deeply ironical and polished analysis of the welfare corporations ations' – V. S. Pritchett), *The Secret Swinger* ('a magisterially wrought comedy that lunges straight for the jugular' – *Book Week*), a philosophical work, *The Immortalist* ('Mr Harrington may have written the most important book of our time' – Gore Vidal) and *Psychopaths*.

ALAN HARRINGTON

The Revelations of
Dr Modesto

Introduction by Vance Bourjaily

PALADIN
GRAFTON BOOKS
A Division of the Collins Publishing Group

LONDON GLASGOW
TORONTO SYDNEY AUCKLAND

Paladin
Grafton Books
A Division of the Collins Publishing Group
8 Grafton Street, London W1X 3LA

Published in Paladin Books 1988

First published in Great Britain by
Andre Deutsch Ltd 1957

ISBN 0-586-08639-0

Printed and bound in Great Britain by
Collins, Glasgow

Set in Ehrhardt

To Roberta Pryor

Introduction

by Vance Bourjaily

The drug of reminiscence grows harder to resist. Persons entering upon their sixties, as I am, all too easily become memory junkies, getting our tenuous highs from the recollection of passions and pleasures long past. But, perhaps because I cannot yet refrain from writing them, I do not find this so with books.

Rereading, occasionally, a book I remember with excitement and affection, I am still more realist than victim of nostalgia, more apt to chide myself for early overestimation than to swoon anew. So it is a pleasure to report that, on rereading Alan Harrington's first novel, *The Revelations of Dr Modesto*, I think it does more than just stand up. My admiration for it has increased.

Let me reminisce after all: 1952 I accepted a short story by Harrington for a periodical called *discovery*. The story (it was probably thrust on my attention by John Clellon Holmes) was the first appearance of this book's central – and, as you will see, centralizing – character, Hal Hingham. It was an account of Hal's failures, built into him from childhood, and of what turned up when he sent seven dollars, in reply to an ad in *Popular Technix*, for a pamphlet called 'The Revelations of Dr Modesto.' Pamphlet, story and, eventually, novel all shared that title.

It was not unusual, in the years just after *discovery*, to see one of the stories I'd chosen for it reappear, developed into a full novel. That was the case with Evan Hunter's story which became *The Blackboard Jungle*; with one by Eliot Asinof, which became *Man on Spikes*; with Chandler Brossard's first chapter for *The Bold Saboteurs*; with a piece of fiction by Anatole Broyard, the *discovery*-story part of which was called 'What the Cystoscope Said.' I don't remember the title of the Broyard novel. There must have been others. My usual experience, when I read the developed book, was a sense of letdown, which I had to recognize as an inability to read objectively. As a magazine editor I was a total enthusiast for every

7

selection I made; as a writer I tended, absurdly, to fantasize that the books to come would somehow sustain and repeat all the characteristics I was so crazy about in the stories. Though I couldn't see it at the time, that this would happen was not merely impossible but totally undesirable.

So when I read *Modesto* as a novel, thirty years ago, I felt that Harrington hadn't done at all what I anticipated; when I reread it recently, I was extremely pleased he hadn't.

My fantasy version would have been, I guess, an ironic, polemical tract, disguised as fiction, with the applications of the Modesto formula for living, centralism, carried out in many episodes – a one-joke book. Ah, how the ingrate author doublecrossed me, writing instead a true novel, with its polemics disguised in as rich a variety of jokes, or call them fictional inventions, as ever Voltaire found for *Candide*.

The most important of Harrington's inventions was, as the reader new to this work is about to discover, Merko, the counter-character to the mysterious, unresponsive Modesto, whoever and wherever he may be.

'"Look around you,"' Modesto's pamphlet recommends. '"And see who is the happy man. He is the one Just Like Everybody Else."'

Hal Hingham may be persuaded by this, but Merko, the Human Fly, scorns being nothing more than the happy man. Even as an adolescent, confronting a psychiatrist, Merko has said, sullenly, '"*I want to be myself.*"'

The psychiatrist trotted out John Donne, '". . . a very wise fellow. He said: 'No Man' – it applies equally to boys – 'No man is an island . . .'"'

'"*Farp,*"' said Merko.

Having stated their positions, each in his own way, neither Modesto nor Merko makes any further effort to claim Hal's loyalty. Hal is left to swing between them, a wandering needle between equally attractive polar opposites. I spoke of *Modesto* as being a work of disguised polemics, but I'd like to change that: it is that item, rare in American literature as some of Melville's shorter works, a novel of ideas.

It deals with the apparent comfort of conforming, the pain and peril of maintaining individuality, and says something quite daring: that, although the nonconformist may or may not ever stop suffering

– it's a matter of luck – the conformist takes the more dangerous road, and will suffer even more.

The means by which this idea – along with several others – is dramatized, are anything but solemn. *The Revelations of Dr Modesto* is in a direct line of traditional comedy, which starts, in English, even before such Elizabethan practitioners as Ben Jonson. It is a kind of comedy that grew out of the ancient, religious morality plays, in which each character represents, and is often named for, a particular trait of character. The signification of Modesto, for example, as a name is clear enough; that of Merko suggests the murkiness of an eccentrically private man. Hal Hingham I take to be named for a particularly average Massachusetts town – in which, as a matter of record, Harrington grew up – and what Joan Vigoro will represent must be clear by now.

Other names may not match up so patly, and still others are more playful than important – as, for example, those of two members of the wonderful Norway Tech backfield, in the brief but climactic football game. They are Skinny Villon and the powerful Poquelin, which was the actual surname of the playwright who signed himself Molière. And even, come to think of it, playful or not, that football game may be taken to comment on Normal vs. Abnormal; the sportswriters figure that the monstrous Bay U. players will overwhelm, by 20 to 0, the small, fast, fragile, mean players from the North.

Presenting these, and many more privately named folks, as he needs them, the writer puts them through an assortment of capers, hijinks and pratfalls, in a burlesque reality that diverts us without ever failing to make its moral points. If that description may be allowed to fit *Modesto*, and I hope it will, it needs to be amplified to point out that, when he chooses to, Harrington can be remarkably subtle as well. I am thinking of the effectiveness of the author's deadpan reiteration of Chapter 12, 'The Love Date,' in Chapter 25, 'The Love Date (2).' The condition of depersonalization could hardly be made more vivid than it is in this devastatingly quiet way – a perfect balance for the vividness of the blatant and equally devastating 'The Rape of Bradford.'

The Revelations of Dr Modesto was Alan Harrington's opening shot as a writer and critic of our times. A friend of Jack Kerouac, as well as of John Clellon Holmes, Harrington traveled with the Beats in the fifties, but was never, it seems to me, a beat writer. His first

9

book, like the many that have followed, is disciplined, organized and economical. Harrington began as an intellectual, rather than as a passionate, writer. If there is controlled passion in the later works, the intellect never falters. I will not try to list them all, but the admirer of *Modesto* may want to read the later novels, from *The Secret Swinger* to *The White Rainbow*, and will find them all rewarding. The same holds for Harrington's works of nonfiction: *Life in the Crystal Palace*, about the business world; *Psychopaths*, which precisely fits its title; *The Immortalist*; and others.

I hesitate, at this point, to make my recommendations any more detailed, or to cite even more books. Like many writers who have been going thirty years or so without much recognition outside the literary community (where Alan Harrington's standing is as high as any), much of the work is out of print and hard to find. This is almost equally true of a number of writers who have had more recognition, as a matter of fact. The failure to maintain the availability of good books is perhaps the sorriest of the several shames in the way American publishing – call it the book business in its abdication from grandeur – presently disserves American letters. All the more reason to be grateful for this reissue of *Modesto*.

Contents

PART THREE

The Revelations of Dr Modesto

PART ONE

1

The Failure

The absent-minded salesman picked his way down the aisle past a double row of desks where the stenographers sat in a long line banging their typewriters. At the water-cooler he paused. He started to his left, then right, and hesitated again. None of the paths before him seemed to lead anywhere. The room was immense, a regular city, and so noisy that he lost all sense of direction. He looked around. A fellow needed a guide, and he thought: 'They ought to have arrows.'

He craned his neck, searching the room with an expression of polite, patient bewilderment, while all around him girls and clerks swarmed in the aisles. Telephones were ringing everywhere. Huge black business machines gave off a steady hum. He imagined a generator under the floor making the business go. Wherever he turned he saw hard-eyed men in shirt sleeves rattling off dictation, girls stapling and stamping and sealing envelopes, tidy old men wrapping and opening packages, and a horde of office boys racing through the labyrinth with more work for everyone.

Even the furniture seemed to be in motion. Rows of desks and filing-cabinets, jammed together at all angles, spread out over the loft in a disorderly spiral. This formation looked as though it were being flung slowly across the room. He imagined that Mr Carmody's business was about to crash through the far wall and burst into space.

He stood and watched the people work. Their industry struck at his confidence, yet he pitied the sullen faces. It seemed to him that there was no life in them; only a purposeless devotion to their jobs. But he had no purpose either, and was hardly qualified to pity anyone.

Resting on a bench, he put his head in his hands. He had a weak impulse to duck out of the interview. He knew what Carmody would be like. Impatient, ham-handed men ran offices of this kind.

He would walk in on a fat face ... He pulled himself together. It was time to get on the ball.

A phone rang near his elbow. It was snatched up by a leathery little man who had torn his collar open, who raked his fingers through his wild hair and shouted: 'No, I won't! Your deadline is Tuesday!' He hadn't meant to stare, but before he knew it the bright, exasperated eyes were fixed on him, and the question was apparently directed at him: 'Well then, what are you waiting for?' Who? He moved away quickly.

He gripped his briefcase and stepped back from the maze streaked now by ladders of sunlight slanting through the venetian blinds. The blaze on the frosted-glass cubicles made him rub his eyes. When he opened them the entire office was illuminated by a dusty glow shot through with sunbeams, and he was surprised to find that a bright, vaguely electric fog lay between him and the job he had to do.

'Who do you want?' demanded an angry voice.

A truculent little bulldog face, fiercely lipsticked, glared at him from under a fringe of bangs.

'Mr Carmody ...'

'Keep right.'

'But where?'

'There!' She pointed to an aisle broader than the others that soon disappeared in the jungle of furniture.

'Thank you very much, I – ' but she simply brushed past him.

He turned to watch her go. She had treated him as though he were carrying packages to the stock room. He wandered on down the broad aisle. He walked through slatted sunlight. Stripes danced on his gray gabardine and touched up the watery shine on his shoes.

He was bumped, and cried out: 'Excuse me!'

The man who had done it called back over his shoulder: 'Sorry, Mac!'

The contact spun him around. He nearly backed into a machine that was throwing a stream of papers into a trough. There was a pretty girl with sun in her hair. She would direct him. He started toward her, but she shut the file drawer, clasped a big folder to her breast, and ran away.

It wasn't intentional; she hadn't seen him. Yet, he knew, there were some people she would have seen. Any of Arcadia's top agents would have captured her eye without effort. Clerks, waitresses, and shopgirls responded to their most casual gestures. They seemed to radiate a worthwhileness that communicated itself instantly to others. He had often tried to imitate their stances and tones of voice, but strangers still walked away from him. His prospects still looked out the window.

He crossed a small clearing and passed some clerks nosing over a field of ledgers. They lifted their heads dazedly. One squinted at him through lenses as thick as eye cups. In spite of his nervousness (the throbbing had already begun in the pit of his stomach), their tired scrutiny made him feel stronger. At least his life wasn't trapped in columns of figures.

He quickened his steps and showed them a slim, fairly good-looking boy about twenty-eight. He had a nice, rather round face weakened by an over-friendly smile. He was of medium height and seemed acceptable at first glance. But he soon gave himself away. An early habit of fear had left a mark on him. He moved cautiously with an instinctive awkwardness, as though aware that his fraud would be discovered at any moment. He winced every now and then in response to some hidden worry. At other times his gray eyes shone wide with a distant focus, and he appeared to be concentrating on imaginary airplanes. He was pale now. His lips puckered anxiously. He gave a faint whistle and stopped to look at something that few salesmen would have bothered to notice.

It was a pencil-sharpener lying on its side; the screws that fixed it to the desk had come loose. He was gazing at it sadly when another girl confronted him. This one had fat arms and a buttery yellow skin, and she said: 'Are you looking for somebody?'

'Yes,' he said, 'but I was just noticing your sharpener. It's too bad when they come apart like that. If I had my tools here – I've got a way of welding them into the desk.'

'Who do you want to see?' asked the fat girl, putting her hands on her hips and staring at him.

'Oh . . . Mr Carmody. I have an appointment.'

'Go straight ahead. No, no, this way. Do you see that door with the transom open? The big door – see it?'

He thanked her, and moved toward the office that could no longer be avoided. He went slowly and more slowly, blinking through the sunbeams. The broken, abandoned pencil-sharpener had depressed him. It reminded him of himself. People didn't care how they treated mass-produced equipment.

He might start an artistic repair business. He had ideas of remaking office chairs and tables into works of art. They would be created especially for reception rooms. He would re-create each piece one at a time with a thousand little painstaking hammerings and carvings, lay golden designs in the flowering wood. At first, naturally, office-managers would resist the idea, and . . . nothing.

His feeble fantasy embarrassed him. He knew why his mind so often took flight before an interview. Rose had put her finger on that. He was running away from reality. Yet sometimes he felt that the things he dreamed of were much more solid than the things he tried to sell.

Even so, he would stop dreaming. He had the will power. He squared his shoulders, but almost at once succumbed to a rush of self-pity. What a monotonous life lay ahead of him! His life was already mapped out, fated. He saw himself in ten, fifteen, twenty years, older and sorrier but otherwise unchanged, a dim figure with a transparent briefcase condemned to wander through hot dusty rooms on impossible errands, and he wondered: 'Why do I have to do it? Who started all this, anyway?'

A woman stepped across his path and looked at him questioningly. The salesman's mild, friendly features underwent a flicker of distress. He forced a smile.

'Boston Chemical?'

'No, I'm Hal Hingham from Arcadia Life. Is Mr Carmody – ?'

'Yes, he's in. I don't think he has much time for you today, Mr Hingham.'

'Well, if he's busy . . .'

'He'll see you, though, I'm pretty sure. Would you wait a moment, please.'

He leaned against the glass partition. He started to put his hat down, but there wasn't any convenient place, so he tucked it under his elbow, meanwhile tugging at the clasp of his briefcase. A breeze rattled the blinds in the long windows, blowing in the clean, sweet smell of the spring afternoon. He thought: 'If I get through soon enough I can take a sunbath.'

The door opened. He heard the secretary answer 'Yes, sir.' It came on and he almost welcomed it, the familiar sinking feeling, not so much of fear as detachment from the ceremony he was about to go through. He knew simultaneously, that he couldn't make good and that he must. Then the whole business became remote. He prepared for a brief dislocation from real life – a prelude to lying in the sun.

He took the booklets out of his briefcase and glanced at them humorously. Sliding his back along the partition, facing with a wan, game smile the banging, bell-ringing typewriters and the purposeful shoutings and comings and goings of everyone in the office-city but himself, he wondered: 'If it's all in the booklets, why do I have to sell it?'

Before he could think any more about that, the secretary nodded to him and said: 'Mr Carmody will see you now.'

2
The Old Story

Hal found himself in a dark room, green-curtained against the noise and sunlight. The carpet he was crossing almost on tiptoe absorbed his footsteps soundlessly. He passed shiny leather chairs, and approached the desk at the far corner of the office. Under the desk lamp he saw, as he had feared, the fat, weary face of a man whose only wish was to be left in peace and quiet.

'Mr Carmody – '

'Just a minute,' said the man behind the desk. He was pawing through an upheaval of papers. After a while he gave up and stared at Hal. It was an angry look, but also a cringing one, as if he expected to be reproved for his defiance. His face was heavy and limp. It seemed enormous because his eyebrows and sparse frazzle of red hair blended to the point of invisibility into his skin. There was something oddly pathetic in his brutal appearance.

'Sir, I'm Hal Hingham, Arcadia Life.'

'All right, sit down. I don't have much time,' Carmody said hoarsely. 'As you see, I'm completely messed up here. I can't seem to do anything right. Why, do you suppose?' he demanded, turning to Hal. 'Do you think I'm sick of this work? Is that what it means?'

'I wouldn't know about that,' Hal laughed. He wasn't going to be sidetracked. 'I do know that a lot of our worries are brought on by concern over the future, and a feeling that we haven't done quite enough – '

Carmody wasn't listening. 'I don't have any feelings any more. I'm just tired,' he said. He began massaging his eyes, and his free hand twitched in his lap. Hal noticed how labored his breathing was. These signs of distress encouraged him. According to the sales manual, one was supposed to create a sense of dissatisfaction in the prospect. Carmody was already unhappy. His anxiety needed only to be directed, for his own benefit, into specific fears of disease, accident, or death.

Hal went on: 'It may be that a complete physical check-up by our doctors might indicate some other condition.'

'If you don't mind, don't talk about it,' said Carmody heavily. He pulled a handful of tissues from a Kleenex carton, and mopped his swollen cheeks. 'I'm not very well. But that doesn't concern me at the moment. I want to know – I wish somebody could tell me – what it's all about.'

'What do you mean, sir?'

'I don't care for anything I do. Nothing makes any difference any more, and I deliberately mismanage. You see – ' Carmody shoveled the pile of papers in front of him, and one went spinning to the floor. 'I let things go, because I feel that these papers are *pushing* me into the corner of a dark room. For what? Can you give me one reason why I shouldn't quit?'

'As a matter of fact, Mr Carmody, we feel that retirement is an advisable goal. Arcadia has a number of policies especially suited – ' He stopped, because the great, aggrieved countenance was regarding him with hostility. 'I'm sorry, sir.' Carmody was a brute wanting to talk philosophy. Life had caught up with him, and now he struggled anxiously to express himself. What a contrast there was between the bustling outer office and the boss cowering within. Yet, after all, it was Carmody's own problem. Hal would have liked to talk philosophy with this unexpectedly decent man, but it was impossible. Time would go by, and he would lose the chance to do any selling.

'Incidentally, I'm insured up to my neck,' said Carmody.

Hal looked down at his notes. 'You belong to the Wompatuck Club, don't you, sir?'

The prospect nodded.

'I guess you know Ken Herbert.'

'Yes.'

'And Bob Arlington?'

'Yes, I do.'

'They took out Arcadia annuities for their kids recently.'

'Fine, but what's that got to do with me?'

'Well, they were in a similar position. They thought they had lived up to their obligations, but they found out that they hadn't completely covered their kids. How about your two boys, Mr Carmody?'

'Look,' Carmody said. His sad, bloodshot eyes blinked under

the light. 'There may be something in what you say. I might even consider it sometime, but don't you understand? There are certain days. You don't care whether school keeps or not. Wife, child, obligations can all go to hell. Didn't you ever have that feeling?'

'No,' Hal said. 'I don't believe I ever did, Mr Carmody. Certainly not with regard to my obligations.'

Carmody looked at him. Hal knew this look. He had experienced it so many times, and now again. The big man was pitying him. There was no more selling to be done, and he stood up. 'I'm sorry to have taken your time,' he said, and walked to the door. He heard the hoarse voice calling his name.

Carmody came out from behind his desk. He made Hal a kind of signal. 'Next time – be human! Don't you have any life in you, boy?'

'Yes, sir.'

'Sell it, then. Sell *life*,' repeated Carmody, and with a distraught grimace he went back behind his heap of papers.

3

Swan Boats at Twilight

He idled by the Explanade and watched some little boys playing with toy sailboats. A boat tipped over, and its owner uttered a series of sad, raucous little cries until his nurse pulled it out for him.

Even though five o'clock had struck, he felt guilty for stopping to look at the children. It was true that no more business would be done. Competition, the pitiless law of life, was suspended until Monday morning. Strong men could go home and relax. They had earned it. He, having earned nothing, ought to be hustling through the emptying office buildings in search of the dollar he hadn't been able to make in regulation time.

The falling sun threw a golden-brown haze over the Esplanade. Pink and gold streamers lay on the river. Along the Cambridge side, windows flashed blinding gold in the apartment houses where the MIT students lived. A gigantic mayonnaise sign already glittered against the smoky northern horizon.

He loafed along for a while. Trying not to think of Carmody's contemptuous face, he turned toward the Common. The cars were jammed together and honking on Charles Street. He jaywalked between bumpers. Somebody shouted at him. In the Public Garden home-going crowds strolled among the banked islands of flowers. They smelled the flowers, studied the Latin labels on the trees, and had their pictures taken by the candid-camera men. Swan boats floated on the pond. Dirty-faced children raced around the edge of the pond yelling at three gentle boys and their nursemaids, who gazed back at them serenely from the swan-boat chairs.

Hal lay down on a slope by an old cannon. Time passed. The afternoon darkened to a warm brown April twilight. A smoke column climbed high over Beacon Hill and hung there for a while before drifting behind the golden dome of the State House. The crowds in the Public Garden were thinning out. Hal sat up against the cannon wheel, still wondering why he had failed to make it with Carmody.

He heard voices. Two girls were lying on the other side of the cannon. Two sailors bent over them with their hands on their knees, each with his hat pushed down over one eye, and cocky, sarcastic smiles sitting on their faces.

'You're fresh,' one of the girls was saying. 'I don't like fresh guys like you.'

'Oh, no? She says she don't like fresh guys like us,' the more aggressive sailor said to his partner. 'That's a coincidence. My mother told me to keep away from bait like you, so how about that?'

'But we're easy to get along with – we don't mind if you don't,' his friend added.

The girl who hadn't objected to anything giggled and hid her face.

'What's so funny?'

'You.'

'Me?' squealed the second sailor, screwing up his face in outlandish agony, and they all burst out laughing.

'I'm fresh and he's funny – that's a good combination,' said the leader of the team, furiously chewing gum and glancing around at several other possibilities even as he made the offer: 'How about going to the Playmor?'

The girls looked at one another.

'Art Christian's there.'

'All right.'

'Well, what are we waiting for? Let's go!' howled the funny sailor.

'So early?'

'Don't worry about that, Josephine.'

'My name isn't Josephine.'

The brutal confidence of the sailors was a mystery to him. He had never dared approach a strange girl, unless Rose counted, and she had really picked him up. He ambled along the path, letting everyone pass him. This was one of his habits that infuriated Rose.

'Hal,' she said, 'you don't even *look* as if you were going anywhere.' Nagged by the sound of her own voice, she tore into him: 'Why do you have to wear your hat perched on top of your head like that?' Once she almost hit him with her handbag. 'Oh, please, can't you stop looking around and sideways and up in the air – and everywhere but *at* somebody? Hal!'

If they were married, she would probably be a lot worse.

He stopped on the bridge to watch the swan boats. A slanting cloud of pigeons whirred down on the bank where an old lady was passing out bread crumbs. She had a little boy with her who squealed and hid his head as the pigeons beat the air around him. Lights were coming on in the office buildings and hotels. Trinity Chimes rang a quarter to six. In fifteen minutes he would be justified in going to supper. He leaned uneasily against the parapet. His eyes were drowsy and gentle. The movement of his lips described the endless conversation he was having with himself.

He was dreaming of a country where peopele walked around happily, never doubting one another. This was possible because there had been an invention, like the lie-detector. It was the character-detector. Everybody carried one. When a decent person touched it, it turned blue.

'Pardon me, buddy, I served in the last one – '

'No,' he said, 'I haven't any money.'

He moved away from the ramshackle old man. Soon it was dark on the bridge. The pigeons on the bank flew off again because the lady had no more bread. The grannies and the little boys abandoned the swan boats. A few people hung around, but when the six-o'clock chimes began they drifted off to supper.

4

A Glimmer of Hope

At ten o'clock, in accordance with the landlady's orders, Hal got up from his workbench and began putting away his tools. This was Mrs Doyle's bedtime, and she refused to let him 'fool around' in her cellar after she was under the covers. Actually he wasn't fooling around at all; he was making things. He liked to make things with tools. It didn't matter a great deal what kind of object he made, as long as he could turn it on his lathe, and hammer, saw, screw, chisel, bore, grind, plane, and sandpaper it. That was the fun of the thing.

He spent most of his free evenings in this damp, rubble-strewn basement of Mrs Doyle's rooming-house. His workbench stood in a clean-swept corner behind the furnace. Light from the bulb outlined a geometry of small shadows on the back wall. These were formed by his works of art – ash trays, cigarette boxes, book ends.

Tonight he had been making funny animals. He wanted one more crack at the top-hatted little duck, to smooth out its tail feathers. His lathe whined softly and stopped, whined again and stopped as a sudden thumping shook the boards of the ceiling. She never gave him an extra minute. He sighed and covered his lathe. The forms silhouetted on the back wall were joined by the shadow of a duck, and he went upstairs.

He had just turned off the light at the head of the stairs when he heard her say: 'Good evening, Mr Hingham.'

'Oh, hello, Mrs Doyle.'

Her bulk blocked the dark hallway.

'Scraping away on a nice night like this?'

'Yes, I've been working.' He didn't like her tone.

'The way you waste these beautiful nights, Mr Hingham – it's not healthy for a boy your age. Why aren't you out with some nice girl?'

'Well, I enjoy – '

' – instead of scraping away on that machine down in my cellar.'

This put him on his guard.

'I don't see why you should object, Mrs Doyle. After all, I pay for using the light. I'm very quiet.'

'Oh, I'm not talking about your noise. It *is* a disturbance, but I mean the shavings.'

'Shavings!' he said. It wasn't fair. He always swept them up.

She was trying to put something over. He wished he dared mutter an excuse and edge by her. He took a step. If she weren't so fat and – inviting with her body. How she panted! He drew back, for she was breathing in his face and the smell of the kitchen on her made him queasy.

'I didn't say anything until now – out of consideration for you. You always seemed like a very nice boy to me. But that business of yours in the cellar is a violation of the fire laws, Mr Hingham. If you dropped a cigarette . . .'

'I don't smoke!' he cried. 'You know I don't. You were hesitating just then – trying to make up reasons,' he told her angrily. 'I keep my wood and tools in an iron box.'

'Didn't you ever hear of spontaneous combustion?' she whispered, and then was seized by a convulsion of the throat. While she coughed and heaved he turned his face to the wall.

She resumed with a deep intake of breath: 'It's dangerous for me – alone every night, with no one to wake me if the house catches fire.'

'There isn't going to be any fire. At least, not because of me.'

'Oh, you can't tell, Mr Hingham.'

'Well,' he said, 'I think I'll – '

'So long as you're a fire hazard I'll have to ask you for five dollars a week more – unless,' she added softly, 'you can find a better way to spend some of your evenings around here.'

He became aware of a great mammal waiting for him in the dark. She made a loose motion. He sensed the tremendous flesh lurking beneath her bathrobe.

'A boy your age,' she said.

She was trying to cheat him. He had a notion to push her fat face in. There was enough to complain about, if he wanted to. No lights on the top-floor landing. Cockroaches. Five dollars a week more! He thought of the luke-warm dribbling shower, the lousy little light bulbs in his room, and the times she had forgotten to change the sheets.

He looked at her. Now his eyes were used to the dark, and the sensual grin he discovered on her face horrified him. He imagined being folded into those overripe arms, and wanted to butt his head against the wall.

'I'll have to let you know,' he said. 'Will Monday be all right?'

'Monday?' She seemed astonished. 'That's up to you, entirely,' she whispered.

The way she was acting, she might jump out of her bathrobe at him. He said: 'Thank you, Mrs Doyle!' and ran past her before she could catch him around the waist. He locked his door.

Night. Fingering through the pages of an old magazine. He sat in a yellow light. His eyes had begun to ache. He bent over a small reading-table with one hand plunged in his hair, squinting at some pictures of office furniture in *Popular Technix*. He turned the page, and another, and yawned.

The room was small and square, with a low ceiling and curlicuing patterns of roses on the wall. He had two chairs, a rocker near the window and the straight-backed one he was sitting on; a sagging, iron-posted bed; and a bureau with a mirror. His window looked out on an alley. The pane was streaked with coal dust. A layer of grit covered the sill. The landlady had sent his curtains to the cleaners a month ago, and the window was still bare. The maroon rug needed cleaning too, but would probably fall apart in the process. Over all this spread the yellow light and a strong smell of cabbage.

He yawned over the back pages of *Popular Technix*. Now the ads: 'Own a Motor Bike.' 'Draftsmen Make Big Money.' 'Be a Detective.' Then something about a Grasshopper Mind. The type was beginning to blur when a headline commanded him: 'STOP!'

He rubbed his eyes and looked again. 'STOP! WHY ARE YOU UNHAPPY?'

'Because I'm different from other people,' he thought dully. 'They don't have any respect for me.' 'FAILURE? TRY CENTRALISM!'

He had seen dozens of these ads before, but this one shouted through his sleepiness. A powerful black forefinger came out of the page, pointing at him. Beneath it was the flat assurance: 'CENTRALISM IS FOR YOU.'

He read:

You're unhappy, uncomfortable, and 'on edge' all the time. The chances are ten to one that you're a FAILURE. How do I know? Because you have read down this far.

'That's true,' he thought, 'you're right. You've got me there.'

Let me reconstruct your situation. At this moment, I suspect, you are alone. You spend a lot of time by yourself. You are poor both in finances and in spirit. You're afraid of people, aren't you?

Yes. His fear was at the bottom of everything. He read on.

I am talking to *you* Mister. You in that lonely room, who wish you could land a date with a pretty girl. You whose palms start perspiring when you're called in for a session with the boss.

Every detail was true. His palms did sweat. 'How does he know?' he marveled. He had a strange feeling of someone imprisoned, waving the key to life, almost hysterically trying to get through to him and help him.

How do I know these things? Because until I discovered Centralism, I was just like you. I was probably even more miserable, more inferior than you are today. Yet practically overnight Centralism brought me *total happiness* and success.

What's the secret? Here's a hint. They cast me out, but I found a way to get back. I didn't fight them. I joined them – with a vengeance!

This is no romance. I positively guarantee that after you have followed a few simple instructions, Centralism will make YOU successful and happy beyond any dream you have permitted yourself.

Unfortunately, space limitations prevent me from disclosing to you the dynamics of Centralism here and now. I will only reveal that my system erases the qualities that make you 'different' from other people. It makes you Absolutely Normal – in a matter of hours. And you will find that this amazing new state of being gives you a STRANGE POWER over others, for no one can *help* loving you.

It was all he had ever wanted – to break out of the awful unattractiveness that made others avoid him. He dreamed of walking down an endless Main Street and being saluted by Tom, Dick, and Harry from gas stations, haberdasheries, and drugstores. He wanted the girls to giggle and gossip with him. He wanted the fellows to take him into their confidence, and when the time came for risky stories he wanted to be in on the laugh. He longed to have someone remark: 'Hal Hingham was there,' as if it mattered.

29

This is a promise, Mister. I offer you *double your money back* in cash if after five short weeks of conscientiously Centralizing yourself you don't find it literally impossible to feel unhappy.

Hal stood up. Common sense told him it would be a waste of money. He tried to forget the wild promise, but, as before, he had the sensation of being shouted at from thousands of miles away. 'FAILURE? TRY CENTRALISM!' The forefinger seemed to rise out of the page and poke at him, insisting: 'FAILURE FAILURE CENTRALISM IS FOR YOU.'

Enclose $7 in cash or money order to cover postage and service charge, and I will send you complete instructions in Centralism by return mail. But hurry! Mail your application TODAY. Don't keep your own happiness waiting.

The message was signed in towering capitals: DR MODESTO. A feathered arrow drew Hal's attention to the coupon below. It came from Box 4508, Broad View, Nebraska. He began filling in the dotted lines.

5

Fred Purdy and the Misfit

Fred Purdy looked at the scared face across the desk and wished that he had not summoned the boy. Death was the only way out for Hingham, or crime. Why try to convince this lump of anxiety that he could sell anything? Because, and only because, it was part of the game, the lifelong as-if. Since all commercial life was a pretense and a fraud, loyalty (to the fraud) compelled him to reassure Hingham: you'll-get-there-yet.

An amiable expression concealed these black thoughts. He was small and dumpy, with a bulbous nose. When he took off his steel-framed spectacles he couldn't see anything. He walked fast on little black shoes, and delighted in his ordinary appearance. Sometimes he observed himself and listened to himself lecturing a group of salesmen and had the ecstatic feeling of being a criminal or a spy in a world full of simple folk. Up the honest bourgeois! Who would suspect his savage disbelief in all the things he lived by?

He pretended to look for something in the drawer. Meanwhile he gave the boy a kindly smile, and felt it seized upon like a bone or a hand to kiss.

'I'm glad you called me up here, sir. I've been wanting to get some advice from you, any . . .'

Misfits annoyed him, because he couldn't have any fun with them. They doubted the same things he did, but instead of laughing at the futility, they cringed. He both scorned and pitied the anxious souls, and the ones who trembled and swore to make good. 'Poor bastards,' he thought. He despised them for their pathetic attempts to conform, yet he was touched by their humiliations. He spoke to them gently ('like a father,' he chuckled in savage amusement) and did his best to convince each one that God had meant him to operate successfully in this lousy world.

'Mr Purdy. I was hoping you could help me.'

'All right, Hingham,' he said. 'Just a minute.'

He pretended to study the contract he had just discovered in the IN basket, and laughed at his aimless chicanery. His blotter was always neat and barren as a putting-green. He had practically nothing to do but sell a little and give pep talks to his underlings. Purdy put down the contract and observed for the first time that the boy was desperate.

'Sir! I want to make a clean breast – '

'Be right with you, Hingham. First, if you don't mind . . .' Purdy excused himself and went off to the men's room.

Hal wanted to make a clean breast of everything. That was the way. Confess. Then everybody made allowances and helped you. He would tell Mr Purdy about his early life – how he was under his dad's thumb and never had a chance to develop. He would insist that he wanted to make good under his own power.

'I'll just throw myself on everybody's mercy,' he decided. This would do at least until he heard from Dr Modesto, if he ever did. Two weeks had passed without a word from Nebraska.

In the men's room the agency-director of Arcadia Life's Commonwealth Branch sat in the middle booth picking sardonically at his own life. He was imagining that he was in jail. He had been put in a cell in this ridiculous position, and in the cells next to him were his business neighbors in similiar travail, everybody under questioning.

'*What do you do, Purdy? What do you really do?*'

'*I write life insurance.*'

'*Apart from the financial gain involved, do you care whether anyone purchases life insurance?*'

'*No, I don't care.*'

'*Who do you really love, Purdy? Your wife and children?*'

'*I have no children, and do not love my wife. Ooh!*'

'*Then what do you really care about, Purdy?*'

'*I like sports. Baseball. The Red Sox.*'

Then came the question he feared.

'*Suppose today all the players on the Red Sox were traded to the Yankees, and all the Yankee players came to Boston in exchange, which team would you be for?*' – *and he didn't know the answer.*

'*But I live as if I care, as if I love!*' *he called after them, laughing, in his own imagination.* '*Give me some credit for that, won't you, boys?*'

Returning to practical matters, he made up the song and dance he would give poor Hingham.

'I guess you know your record. You haven't got one,' he said. 'You haven't sold anything since I can remember. If it wasn't that your father had been with the company, we'd have thrown you out.'

'I know it. I lack confidence, Mr Purdy!'

'Incompetent selling . . . reflects on us . . .'

'Yes! That's just what I wanted to talk to you about!'

Purdy saw in Hingham's earnest young face the lust to confess. 'Tell me about it, son,' he said.

'Well, my father died five years ago. He was good to me, in a way. He even left me a little income. But I think I've still got a complex about him. I've got to get away from it if I'm ever going to make a success, Mr Purdy. I've thought about it a long time,' Hal went on, encouraged by his boss's nod of sympathy.

'I've been leaning on the reputation my dad made here at Arcadia, and it's bad for me. It's really a handicap, because I'm always comparing myself with him, and so does everybody else . . . You see, he was a fine man, all right, but not much of a father to me. I mean he never paid much attention . . . My mother died when I was born, Mr Purdy. I was brought up by my Aunt Mary – she's my dad's sister. I never had much chance . . .'

He told Mr Purdy how it was with his gloomy boyhood in Hampton, how his dad stayed away for months at a time. He – frightened by the other boys – would, for example, vainly challenge Aunt Mary to play baseball. He played alone with dolls and trains in the hot attic. His father appeared one day only long enough to drag him, kicking and screaming, into the Boy Scouts.

'Yes,' said Purdy to himself, 'you are an unfortunate weakling,' as Hingham confided and confessed and pleaded, flinging open all the doors and windows of his childhood.

The boy had a father complex as big as a house. Samuel Hingham was supposed to have been a stuffy and dominating individual. Even so, that was no excuse. You had to choose the right parents – or else.

'I've got to stand on my own feet!' declared young Hingham.

'Of course,' his boss agreed. 'You've got the right idea, son.'

'I thought of changing my name.'

'Well, that might help you. Perhaps it would be better, though, if you could learn to live with your name, and use it.'

He was bored and disgusted with his own counsel, especially since he knew that Hingham was not really listening to it. Like all weaklings, this one was tyrannical and also dishonest. Whining, they challenged the great as-if that was necessary to keep things going. Hypocrisy was not good enough for them.

'Listen,' he said angrily. 'What do you come to me for? You don't believe in your job. Why should you? It's utterly unimportant. So don't believe in it. I'll tell you something, Hingham. Unbelief is a wonderful thing – it frees a man for action.'

'What, sir?' said Hingham, shaken.

'I say getting ahead isn't important. Nothing's important.'

'I'll make good, Mr Purdy,' Hal promised. He wanted to get out.

'And now that you've heard my opinion, disbelieve it. Do you follow me?' Purdy's smile followed him.

'I – '

'*Pretend* to believe, or you'll fail.'

As Hingham stumbled out, the phone rang.

'No, dearest,' Purdy said. 'I'm going to be very late tonight.'

This time, for some reason, the lie distressed him.

'No, no, dear. You can't phone me where I'm going to be.'

The faded serene face he couldn't see, the gentle disappointment in her voice, made him wince.

'Sure, I'll call you.'

How many nights he left her alone.

'Don't wait up, now. You need your beauty sleep. Good-bye, darling,' he said miserably, as if lying were a sin.

6

A Message from Nebraska

After eating gray hamburgers at Vathek's cafeteria, Hal hurried along under the lamps of Marlborough Street, half-walking, half-running to get home to bed. The interview with Purdy had exhausted him. He imagined running on until he fell or disappeared in the darkness.

Small worries raced through his mind. He had no prospects lined up. He was nearly broke for the week, and had no idea how he was going to pay the extra rent Mrs Doyle wanted. This painful question reminded him that she might be listening for him in the hallway. He would have to step softly.

Miserable years extended before him, and he saw no escape from his cringing existence. An old despair took hold of him. He had first suffered from it in Hampton – the fear that he was the wrong combination of his ancestors, a runt whom no amount of training would help. He remembered another fragment of his childhood, swinging vainly at a great furry ball, and the grief-stricken tennis-instructor his father had hired splintering his racket across his own flanneled knees and roaring at him: 'You're unco-ordinated!' Yet eventually he had learned to play a fair game of tennis. His unco-ordinated personality could be trained too, as the man from Nebraska had promised. But where was Dr Modesto's guaranteed Answer to Life? Either lost in the mail or a fraud.

He walked unsteadily into a soft wind. The street-lamps flung his silhouette away from him. He walked past the lace-curtained windows of Marlborough Street and came to a house. There they were again, every night – three ladies under enormous fringed lamps playing cards with an old man. They played against a backdrop of an emerald screen, dragon tapestries, and silver dust that seemingly exuded from the walls. Tonight the tableau frightened him. The ladies reminded him of his aunt, and the feeble old man of himself some day. He ran on, fearful of his future.

Who helped an impotent man? It was useless to appeal to Rose: 'I can't make it, comfort me.' Girls refused to accept certain confessions. He could hear her:

'Hal, if the others can sell life insurance, so can you. You just haven't gone about it in the right way.' She would seize his limp hands, and explain sadly yet impatiently: 'You aren't really *trying*. You don't put your *mind* to it.'

He saw her bright eyes; the thin, angled arms, and her tense body line of bones and tendons and energy. There was no refuge in her lap. She was metallic and penetrating, he thought, like the X-ray machines she handled.

He closed the front door softly behind him.

There was a big white envelope on the hall table lettered 'CENTRALISM IS FOR YOU.'

It was like getting ready for his bride. First he turned his bed down and laid the envelope across the pillow. He took a fresh white handkerchief from the bureau drawer and began dusting things. Soon his luxuriously slow movements excited him.

He undressed and crossed the hall to the bathroom. Several minutes later, still moist from his fast, cool shower, he jumped into bed. He opened the envelope.

The pamphlet that fell out was entitled 'THE REVELATIONS OF DR MODESTO.'

The Revelations of Dr Modesto

The Confessions of Dr Modesto (1)

I was born more than fifty years ago in the state of M—. My father was the minister of a mild faith. Although our denomination was not strong in numbers, it happened that a large percentage of the national membership was concentrated in the southwest corner of M—. This circumstance allowed my father to boast (something he never did) of more parishioners than attended the Roman Catholic and Protestant churches in the vicinity. But, as I say, he would never have dreamed of boasting about anything. He was proud of his meekness and cherished it, happily knuckling under to anyone who challenged him.

My mother was, if possible, an even less vigorous person than he. She seldom spoke out loud. When she did give voice to one of her harmless thoughts, you generally couldn't hear her. If she were asked: 'What's that?' she would go into paroxysms of embarrassment. My father and I never made this mistake. It was not unusual for my mother to murmur all through dinner without our interrupting our own conversation or hearing a word she said.

I was an unobtrusive boy. The shouts and squabbles of childhood had no meaning for me. I passed mildly among the other boys, waiting patiently for the time when I would be grown-up. Surprisingly enough, although I was the minister's son, they didn't pick on me unduly. I seemed to baffle them.

At one point – I think I was fourteen – they did try a strange trick on me. They pretended I was invisible. They would walk at me as if there was nothing but air where I stood, and they would bump into me. The game was to look frightened and then enormously relieved: 'Oh,' they would say, 'it's you! Why don't you let people know you're there?' I accepted all this without complaint, without breaking into tears as they probably expected. Gradually the game was discontinued – or perhaps it never was. I used to wonder whether I really had become invisible in the course of the joke, because thereafter they noticed me so little *without trying*.

I didn't care. I was devoting myself to religious studies. It was assumed that I would follow in my father's footsteps and some day 'inherit' the parish. I pored over his sermons and kept a notebook, jotting down thoughts of my own that seemed instructive yet not too aggressively challenging. Watching him at parish teas and picnics, I saw that he had managed to win something like respect for his meekness – even from those who slapped him on the back and joked with him about holding the softest job in the county – a reference to his working only one day a week.

For my part, I'm afraid I didn't love or admire him very much. I wanted to, but I found myself wishing that he threw a longer shadow – so that I could feel at least a little bit dominated by him. He and I seemed to have milk in our veins, and I suppose I blamed him for passing his *unimpressiveness* on to me. Yet I believed in his good life. I had to, because my life would be the same. Or, rather, it would have been the same if the stranger with the books had not struck our town without warning the week after my seventeenth birthday.

It was a hot, damp midsummer afternoon. I was walking as usual in the direction of the library when I heard jingling sounds and the clatter of hooves. There were shouts from Main Street. I ran toward them. A crowd had gathered in front of the general store. Everyone was gaping at a gaudy caravan fringed in gold like a circus wagon. A white horse stood in the traces, whisking its tail. Fiery letters blazed out from this spectacular vehicle: MAYNARD THE ATHEIST.'

Then I saw a cruel-looking zealot mounted on the steps of the van. He had a dark, passionate, scornful face and long black hair. He was passing out green booklets and shouting through a megaphone, haranguing us with wild, strange phrases. I pressed closer to hear what he was saying. Soon I was shocked and frightened. I saw fear and anger on the faces of my neighbors.

He was challenging any religious leader of our town to debate the existence of God.

Of course, the constable was sent for. But our savage visitor was prepared for this. Shaking his fist, he laughed. 'You call the police because you're afraid! A typical lot of believers you are. You're afraid, that's what it is. You know your feeble faiths can't stand up

to my arguments, and once you listen to me you'll *all* be atheists –
yes, *all* of you!'

At this the crowd began growling and moving toward him, but
he wasn't in the least intimidated. He went on flailing his arms and
taunting us. Now and then he would throw out a shower of green
books, which already some unthinking people had picked up and
begun to read.

Suddenly a voice came out of the crowd: 'Stop! Don't injure
him!' I was amazed to see my father push his way through the
multitude and stand before the atheist.

'I will accept this man's challenge!' he said.

Immediately everyone was cheering my father. I wish I could say
that he cut a noble figure, but the truth is that there was an
expression of such vacuous complacency on his face that I could
hardly bear to look at him. The atheist, who stood about a foot
taller, grinned down hungrily at my father. As the townspeople
cheered, I prayed to God for His Own sake to produce another
champion – someone, almost anyone else, to combat the fierce
unbeliever who had so abruptly burst into our lives.

Unfortunately, there was no Divine intervention. Father Dono-
van of the Roman Catholic Church was in the hospital. The
Episcopal minister, Father Lawrence, had gone to the state capital.
It was arranged that my poor father would debate Maynard the
Atheist at the grange hall that same evening.

Torches flared on the stage. Rafters trembled, windows rattled,
the beams of the hall shook from the tattoo of stamping feet. An
ovation greeted my father. 'Bring on the atheist!' we cried, and
then he came, and there was a vast silence, for the two made a
terrifying contrast on the speakers' platform. My father sat with his
hands folded, and a melancholy yet insufferably complacent smile
on his lips. The stranger, utterly unafraid of us, came striding
onstage with a suitcase full of those books, which he promptly
unpacked and spread out before our eyes. Then he surveyed us in
a lordly way – (we who could have carried him out of town astride
a piece of kindling from his own caravan) – and he looked at us
almost pityingly, as if he regretted having to cram the truth into so
many foolish heads.

We waited for someone to call the debate to order. Maynard
strode about the stage, looked at his watch, then at my father, and
suddenly he leaped, actually leaped across the platform and cried

out: 'Do you contend, Mr Minister, that a personal God exists somewhere in the sky?'

'I do, sir,' replied my father. 'Otherwise I should not be here.'

'And ... And!' the atheist's voice came howling through our applause. 'He sent down His only begotten Son to speak for Him, eh?'

'Well, in a manner of speaking,' said my father, our faith not being too insistent on this point. 'Yes, and – '

'Then the Son we may suppose had *faith* in the Father?'

'Of course.'

'Well, then!' shouted Maynard, flourishing his whiplike arm in my father's face. 'Let's hear you tell your flock what Jesus said at the last moment!'

'Why, surely,' my father began. 'You mean – '

'You know where I mean,' sneered the atheist.

My father opened his mouth, but no words came. His face took on a ghastly hue. I cringed at the pathetic sight, and hid myself in the crowd.

Looking back, I don't know ... I think perhaps the invasion of our town by this man was heaven-sent to test the mild faith we held. At any rate, Maynard's juvenile arguments that any courageous schoolboy might have answered threw us into confusion.

When my father finally mumbled what Jesus had said, the atheist exultantly pounded his fist into his palm.

'Exactly! In other words, even *he* lacked faith. At the end, mind you – that's when most people really believe – he abandoned his faith completely.'

'Which shows that he was human, even as you and I,' said my father in a trembling voice.

'Human, eh?' laughed Maynard, winking at us as though we were on his side. 'All right, but still you admit my point. *He changed his mind at the last moment.*'

'Well – '

'Did he or did he not, according to Scriptural authority, change his mind?'

'He did,' my father whispered.

'Then who in heaven's name are *we* supposed to have faith in?'

A murmur of anger went up all over the hall. We turned to my father, waiting for him to speak out and destroy the spurious argument, but he remained slumped against the speakers' table. It

42

seemed to me that he was eyeing Maynard the Atheist in a sort of ecstasy, craving punishment from him like an ancient martyr.

From that moment on he offered only token resistance to this logic-chopping lawyer of the devil. What objections he did make were like offerings to the brutality of Maynard's assault on all that he held dear.

'How do you explain the soul in the light of recent developments in quantum mechanics?'

'What was that?'

'Quantum mechanics! I presume you know what *they* are.'

'No,' said my father, 'I've never heard of them.'

'Bah!' the atheist laughed. 'And how do you account for the lungfish?'

'I beg your pardon?'

'We know that inbreeding produces idiocy. Why are not all Noah's descendants, presumably including ourselves, congenital idiots if – '

'You know, sometimes I think we are,' said my father ruefully.

This frail joke gave us something to cheer about, but not for long. Maynard shot his finger at my father's nose and demanded: 'Could God make a mountain so big that even *He* couldn't move it?'

And my father couldn't answer him. I don't want to think about that evening any more. It is enough to say that he was humiliated many times over. We heard him yield up his beliefs, one after another. The difference was – I could have sworn – that while we suffered he was enjoying it. His eyes were closed. An agonized smile played on his lips. At times his body would jerk ecstatically as some especially humiliating admission was forced from him.

Finally Maynard gave a great roar of laughter. He flung my father one last scornful glance, picked up his suitcase, and, pivoting like a discus-thrower, hurled armloads of booklets at us. As we scrambled for them, he kissed us off with an arrogant gesture of farewell and swaggered out of our lives. A few minutes later my father was left alone in the hall, a broken and ridiculous figure.

I am told that only five people came to church the following Sunday. They found no minister on duty. My father had simply disappeared, and he was gone for a month. The strain, I know, hastened my mother's death. When my father finally did return (from the slums of the state capital, we discovered later) he had become unrecognizable. He smoked and drank a great deal. He walked about the house with a dreamy smile, talking to himself. The night my mother died, and the neighbors came, he would not stop chuckling. Then he was sent away . . .

The Confessions of Dr Modesto (2)

How they picked on me! I mean the people of the town – as if I were responsible for my father's fiasco. Children were instructed to laugh at me on the street. On Halloween they piled tin cans on my front walk. At night I could hear their angry laughter outside my window.

To imagine what an effect these events had on me, remember that I was a shy and inhibited boy under the best of circumstances. I never doubted that I had been placed on earth to continue my father's work. I had fitted myself for a career in the pulpit rather than the market place, enduring 'invisibility' games and such in order to achieve the meekness I needed. Then all at once my future was destroyed by the scandal.

Maynard not only ruined my father; he had contaminated me. I believed in nothing. I was prepared for nothing. Who was I? 'I am Jesus' little lamb, Jesus Christ, how glad I am.' That's what the children shouted after me – under the *instructions* of their parents, I know. The conspiracy almost dehumanized me. I began to feel like a queer and inadequate fish, sick of water and unfit for land – a mutation, a specimen of humanity somehow gone wrong. Yet I had to make my own way. For the first time I realized that the outside world was a place of mysterious brutality.

I sold the little house where I had expected always to live, and traveled to the state capital. There an old schoolmate of my father found me a job writing articles on religious subjects for the *National Encyclopedia*. At first this seemed like a wonderful position, perhaps the only job in the world I could hope to do with any degree of competence. Unfortunately, my lack of enthusiasm showed in my work. Some of the articles I turned in had sneering, skeptical overtones that affronted the *Encyclopedia* editors. Even more important was the tone of my personality.

The hammerings of society had made me, as I say, strange. The

45

son of a disgraced father, I was continually tormented by the fear that I might disgrace myself at any moment. I developed nervous mannerisms, blinking, coughing, swallowing; my palms sweated. My voice trembled in the presence of my superiors. And everyone, it seemed, was my superior.

I tried desperately to get on an equal plane with people, but I always failed. It was uncanny. No sooner did I enter a room than every man and woman in the place *instantly* sized me up as an unimportant person. Somehow, in some strange way (I thought), they all sensed my 'difference.' No matter what I did – or how I tried to say the right thing – they would glance at me casually, then turn away and go on talking to someone else.

The peculiar relationship I'd had with my boyhood acquaintances – of being invisible to them – was repeated now in my early manhood. People were always *bumping into me.*. The more inconseqential I was, the more embarrassed I became. Inevitably, I was fired, or the next thing to it. Out of respect for my father, his old friend let me try selling encyclopedias from door to door.

This was the beginning of a miserable life for me. I walked from one end of the city to the other, staggering under the weight of all those books, dropping them, picking them up wet and dirty, having to pay for the damaged volumes, lugging them to a door and then, as the housewife peered out, dropping them. I was repulsed always. Day after day with all the world's knowledge in my arms, I couldn't sell a single volume.

I fled through the years, stumbling from one job to another. My savings were used up. I went down and down the social scale. With each new job I became more timid and unprepossessing. I worked at lunch counters, cleaned kitchens. Finally I was clean-up man at an animal hospital. One day just before lunch the superintendent came up to me and said: 'I have bad news for you!' I shouted at him: 'Oh, no! I quit! I quit!' I rushed into the street.

It was a lovely blue noon. I will never forget that day. The sun seemed to bathe the sidewalk and all the people with a bright godly balm. God seemed to have relented and forgiven me (and everyone) all sins that could possibly be committed. I imagined a healing power in the soft sunlight. Desperation left me. I gazed at my fellow men and women passing by and suddenly I wasn't afraid of them.

I thought: 'Here I am, a lonely and unattractive man on a street corner. Why is this? What is it that prevents me from becoming everybody's comrade?' I didn't ask the question resentfully. I was in a dreamy mood. I said to myself: 'If I could only be in the middle of them all,

> looking the same,
> feeling the same,
> and believing the same

things they do – if I could be *just like everybody else*, no more harm and suffering would come to me!' It had started as a reverie, but now the idea took violent hold of me.

I longed somehow to be able, by an act of will, to disappear into that crowd, and emerge after a while with an absolutely common face, a new presence, a new soul even – to be *not myself* any more, but somebody else. Or *everybody* else, the average person!

All my misery and 'apartness' was a result of wandering about the edges of life, of being different from others. If it were possible to find out what people *were* in the average – and place myself in the exact center of the crowd and become The Average Fellow . . .

Oh, heaven! I was laughing. If I could! If a rejected man could reject himself, abandon the self that others despised, and simply melt into them all! What was stopping me? Why couldn't I step out of my *self* and walk away from 'it' – just begin to walk?

I heard a rushing sound like wings and thought I was swooning away.

I remember. I was in the exact center of town. I was staring at a brick wall, particularly at the central brick on my eye level. This brick. It blocked up the corners of my mind. Six inches from my eyes, it was rough, red, porous, slashed by a nail someone had dragged across the surface. And I was thinking: 'We're all particles, the same.' In sameness there was strength, what held us together . . . I felt vaguely that my mind was losing me, that I was separating from myself, drifting off. My identity was *disappearing* into this rock. What was I? Clay. An extension of dust, accidentally assembled, soon to fall apart. A form among infinite forms mingling together and vanishing. Drawing my anonymity about me like a cloak, I started to walk.

All that day I walked about the city. I was (although I didn't know it then) taking the Centralist's Walk – nearly asleep, yet alive as no normal waking man has ever been. I was not exactly directing myself. Better say I gravitated here and there, overhearing voices, spying gestures, turning my look on the faces of everybody else. I loitered in cafeterias, idled through parks, in office buildings and hotel lobbies. I stalked the poor and rich sections. I went everywhere, listening, watching . . . Nothing escaped me. Nor did anyone notice me. They never guessed that a human calculating-machine was loose among them totaling up their composite state of mind, and that I was forming my new character from the *average* of theirs.

I had to take the Centralist's Walk to do this. I had to be nearly asleep. The way I was, I saw them in slow motion. They came drifting toward me. I could see into everything that was going on in their minds, and I could divine the hidden meanings behind what they said to each other. I entered into the spirit of each person who walked by. I lost my *self* in the mass, and joined it forever.

I fell into an ecstasy of mediocrity. Whatever the others did, I did. Whatever they thought and wanted, I thought and wanted. Casually, I batted the breeze with strangers and found that my trivialities were welcome. I was rocked by waves of happiness as I realized and realized that I (or the identity I had taken on) was no different from anyone. 'But who am I? What am I?' I cried out, suddenly panic-stricken by the thought that it was getting dark. I would soon have to go to sleep, and perhaps I would wake up my old self. My escape from that wretched condition had been accidental. I had somehow gone to sleep on a street corner and become new. Would I be able to manage it again?

It had begun to rain. I decided to rush home and write down everything that had happened to me, noting the smallest details. In this way I would be sure to remember – but I had to hurry!

My streetcar rolled clanging past leaping, protesting figures. 'Express!' the motorman was exclaiming angrily. 'Express, damn you! I got my orders.'

I was looking, I thought, out the window when all of a sudden I discovered something printed *in* the glass. You know the transparent chains that sometimes swim across your eyeballs. These chains, mingling with raindrops, were forming a kind of structure along the pane. There was a single raindrop in the center of the pane. It was surrounded by a network of transparent chains, and as the chains descended, so did the drop, keeping the formation perfect, the raindrop *centralizing* itself, I thought, and then I had it – only a word, but The Word, expressing it all:

Centralism

I jumped from the trolley while it was still moving. I ran home, treasuring the discovery in my mind. I ran upstairs, and seized pencil and paper. Then I had a vision.

I was looking at a city. Above the buildings and towers floated a sphere, like a halo, representing the community soul. The sphere was not perfect, nor was it constant. It kept varying slightly, bulging here and hollowing there. But it was roughly a sphere.

I observed people walking in the city, and most of them had the same kind of spherical halos floating over their heads. At times a wave of 'popular opinion' would alter the shape of those little spherical selves. Then the large form that floated above the city would be similarly altered. Basically, though, among the more normal (and therefore happier) people, general sphericity prevailed.

But there were those whose souls were triangular. They walked the streets in wretchedness. They were snubbed and humiliated and kept in a state of chronic unemployment, because their souls did not *fit in* with those of the regular people. The more triangular they were, the more they suffered. Some were capable of bending slightly, and their misery was relieved from time to time. But those who were rigidly and psychopathically triangular burst into tears or shot themselves.

I drew closer, and the city dissolved into many cities. Everywhere I saw hundreds and thousands of men and women with triangular selves struggling hopelessly through life. I was filled with a vast and understanding pity for them. 'Must this be?' I thought angrily. 'Must we, through no fault of our own, suffer from the eternal 'Abnormality' laid upon us?' (For as I watched the army of misfits crying in the streets, I observed that some selves were born 'abnormal,' while others were subsequently twisted into ugly shapes – as mine had been – by force of circumstances.)

'But now,' I thought, 'I CAN SAVE YOU ALL.'

The Confessions of Dr Modesto (3)
The Doctrine of Centralism

1. Since your self grates on others, and makes you miserable, get rid of it.

2. In our society, in our time, it does not pay to be yourself. People laugh at you and call you strange – even if it was your father's fault.

3. Look around you, and see who is the happy man. He is the one Just Like Everybody Else. 'Oh, so that is the way to be?' you ask, and I say, yes, that is the way you and I must be.

4. You are a sensitive person in a world of Brutes. Like a feeble animal, you need protective coloration. You must hide.

5. The only place to hide is in the center of their culture. Be more average than anyone!

6. From this moment on, HAVE NO SELF.

7. Have no mind of your own. Have no thought, opinion, habit, no desire or preference, no enthusiasm, love, or fear of your own. *Be* the composite of your neighbors.

8. When you have not a shred of individuality left, no one can clash with you. Once you reach this state, it will be *absolutely impossible* for you to be unhappy.

9. You wonder again, anxiously: 'Is this the way to be?' and I say, yes. What other chance do we have? Because we are sensitive and 'different,' they pick on us. They set Brutish standards, and call us misfits for not measuring up to them. To survive, we must become happy nothings.

10. We'll form a massive nothing in the heart of the United States of America, and operate from there.

II

11. This is the way you melt into the Community Mind: STARE AT ONE OBJECT. For instance, you might choose an awning or a drain pipe. Stare at it until you lose yourself. Then begin the Centralist's Walk through the streets.

12. It is an unusual sensation. There will be a hush all around you. Hear the people. All the faces have bright eyes. Their voices come through the uproarious silence and whisper in your ear. You will obtain an instantaneous fix on many lonelinesses. Louts meditate for you. A cry of anxiety rings out of a horselaugh.

13. After a while, all the ideas that inhabit the town inhabit you.

14. When the sleepwalk is over, you wake up The Central Man in town. There is a moment when the intolerable burden of self is lifted from you. Oh, if you could only *know* how it feels to be free of caring about anything. Drifting along in the center of the crowd, you are utterly happy. Peace radiates from you, making others happy. And this gives you practically limitless power over others!

15. It is the power of averageness. Nobody can resist you. How could they? You are the Norm around which their own lives are arranged. They are completely centralized by you. Without knowing it, they want to yield to you, because each one sees himself in your image, and they all love you as they love themselves.

III

16. The Central Man comprehends all variations from the average, including the extremes, because they went into forming him. Thus, he can centralize the wildest hermit or the dullest clerk, and make them love him and buy whatever he has to sell. The hermit will detect a brother wild man; the clerk will respond to the image of a fellow clod. The Centralist assumes either of their identities at will. He does so automatically. But he has no personality of his own, for this is the very condition of his happiness.

17. Remember that in yourself you are nothing. This means that you cannot be alone too long, for then you will have no one to 'be.' If you do not see people, you may faint and forget, and the vestiges of your old, permanent self will drag at you and pull you back toward your former state.

18. Realize that your initial happiness is not permanent. You will have to practice for quite a while, and melt into all kinds of towns, before you can adjust effortlessly to any circumstance.

19. One rule will protect you – make the idea of Centrality a fixation. Maintain a fanatic devotion to the center of everything. LIVE CENTRALLY. Even this. Live as close as possible to the geographical center of town. There is no joking. The idea should permeate everything you do. Pursue it to any lengths – your position in a group photograph, your seat in a bus. Such apparently meaningless acts add up to one dominating reflex, so that eventually – even when there is no pleasure or point in doing so – you will take your place in the center, where no harm can come to you.

20. I also tell you BELIEVE and THINK CENTRALLY, which is to say believe in nothing, but give your loyalty to any popular cause in the vicinity. And give it precisely in half-measure, depending on what your neighbors believe. If they despise a certain race, join moderately in the pleasures of contempt. But then, supposing a liberal element comes to town, trim your position. You have to adjust, like a wire-walker carrying a long pole, who keeps his eyes on the dips and lifts of the pole ends, and takes warning from them in time to maintain his balance. So, when the liberals come, your old position is slightly unbalanced, and you change your beliefs. Say, perhaps: 'There are some good ones.' With the arrival of more leftists, cite scientific evidence of the equality of races.

21. If this disturbs you, I will go further. I tell you, you have no morals any more. Prepare to do good and beautiful things and monstrous things. You will love God when you are with good people. But if some Maynard comes into your life, you will not be afraid to deny God and drink toasts to the death of God with a townful of atheists, for you *are* not religious and you *are* not an atheist. You are both and neither. Just as you are a moderate drunkard among drunkards. Or if you are a prison guard, you will be just as brutal as the others. But I can see you in the time of the great floods. When the Red Cross atmosphere is everywhere, and the newsreel cameras take pictures of heroes risking their necks to get people down off the housetops, you will be in one of those boats with a baby safe in your arms.

22. I say also, I will go further. When I took the Centralist's Walk in the city of M—, I saw some oafs teasing a waitress, and I *believed* then in teasing helpless girls, and I joined them (rough men who would normally have frightened me), and by making insulting remarks to the waitress I made them love me, and they begged me to go bowling.

23. Now you are beginning to see the conditions of your happiness, and the power you will have. You will think in the center, and be ready to delight in trivialities. Care which team wins. Spend hours comparing the kinds of gasoline that all come from the same pipeline. Every time you wash your car it always rains, if that's the general story. Throw salt over your shoulder. Knock on wood.

24. You will also BEHAVE CENTRALLY. This means that for every man you talk to, the air becomes a mirror. And every woman sees in you the kind of man who *rests* her at that moment. That is your secret. You *rest* people, often – especially in a group – without their being aware of you. At any party you are the fellow getting ice cubes. You're 'around,' virtually invisible, yet the gathering revolves about you. When you leave, a great nervousness may fall on everyone.

25. I tell you to WORK CENTRALLY. Despite your power to make anyone do your bidding, you should not rise to the top. Get ahead, but moderately. Work at a typical job for an ordinary salary. The extremes of worldly success and failure are equally dangerous, because they throw you off-center. Failure begets worry and the poor opinion of others. Success creates prominence and the envy of others. Both prevent your remaining Central.

26. PLAY CENTRALLY. Never be a champion. In tournaments lose out deftly in the middle rounds. You will know the joys of coming in second when the chips are down. Remember that the champion is a plaything in your hands. He will flourish and die, but you will endure. When all the tournaments are over (because everyone must have the same ability), you will have your day.

27. Finally, you must abandon Love. Is this a sacrifice? I ask you, how can you love? For you, love is the last enemy – a terrible, unbalancing, uncalculated thing, ruinous to the peace of mind, destroyer of urbanity, a most individual process of *caring* that will end you, I warn. The Centralist *practices* love, but cannot for one unguarded moment permit it in his heart. He is the virtuoso of love, who can produce greater, shall I say, amounts of love, of the highest quality – greater than the sickliest-hearted worshipper – yet, for his survival, feel none of it.

28. I come to the FINAL EQUILIBRIUM, and ask you, savagely, is this sacrifice too much? Or would you rather return to the 'individual' state, and have them sneer and laugh at you, and give you dirty clean-up jobs in animal houses? Go back, then! I assure you, they are waiting, *poised* to ignore you.

29. My enemies will say to you that Centralism is unprincipled, but I demand: 'Where are *their* fabulous principles, in so far as they ever applied to *us?*' We bring encyclopedias to their doors. What principles prevented all those doors from slamming in our earnest faces? Oh, no! We know their world. *Science* is disproving all their principles, and showing that they are nothing. All their prophets had bad sex lives. All through history, it's not what you know, but who you know.

30. Listen. Modest, safe, and sure. That's the way to power. Are you afraid of obscurity? But, my boy, my son, we will be everywhere. All of us, running things. Only give your *self* up. Come with me, and together we will infiltrate back into the world that rejected us.

Dr Modesto

7

A New Life

The moon discovered a shape thrashing beneath its cover of sheets and blankets. Presently Hal struggled from the bedclothes and stood up. He stretched his arms, gave a long shudder, and relaxed. Then with careful dreamlike movements he began to dress. He put on his hat. Coat hangers jingled as he went out, closing the door behind him.

He went dreamily downstairs and on down to the cellar. He stayed there about ten minutes. When he emerged he was clutching an iron box and a duffel bag filled with assorted works of art. A duck's head, protruding comically through a hole in the canvas, waggled with his every step.

He ambled into the warm midnight of Marlborough Street. Carrying his burdens to the corner, he gently laid the box and bag in the trash barrel.

Then he returned to his room and started, in the middle of the night, to pack his suitcases.

8

Exterminator at Work

The exterminator found out about Hal Hingham, and wished he hadn't. He visited Mrs Doyle's rooming-house on the first and fifteenth of each month to knock off cockroaches wherever he found them, which was inevitably in all the bathrooms and in the landlady's kitchen. He came also for his pleasure – that is, for a couple of years now it had been his custom to climax the tour of duty upstairs with a fast five minutes of love with the lady of the house. He had stumbled on this bonanza; or, rather, it had sandbagged him, he said, 'out of no place.'

He looked as though he had been heaped out of yellow-brown clay, massive above the waist in the mold of a hero, with an outcropping of biceps and triceps that kept his arms perpetually bowed out from his sides. Unfortunately the rest of him fell away to a pair of straggly short legs. His head too was an apologetic afterthought for a hero. The mouse-colored hair swept to a point. His horn-rimmed glasses, contracted brows, and sallow, stubbly skin gave him a submerged appearance, as if he had abandoned all joys, excepting one, and given over his life to the endless labor of exterminating cockroaches. His face lighted a bit, though, when he told his friends what had happened the first time he poked his head into Mrs Doyle's gloomy hallway and yelled: 'Exterminator!' before going upstairs.

It was the goddamndest thing, he said. He had just finished with the kitchen when she claimed she'd seen roaches in the bedroom and wanted him to use his squirt gun in there. She'd been floating along with him up and down all the floors like a big white logy balloon, bumping up against him and practically falling out of her dress when she bent over, but he hadn't thought anything of that. Sometimes when their husbands were away they liked to fool with you, but it was more or less to be sociable, and how was he to know that Old Man Doyle had been dead for eighteen and a half months?

Anyway, he was kneeling and firing under the bed at nothing he could see but dust when all of a sudden he felt a tremendous soft weight bearing down on him, and she was kissing him behind the ears saying she just had to . . . Before he knew it he was sprawled on the bed (still holding his cockroach gun) and rolling around with a two-ton earthquake, and trying to breathe through explosions of kisses like – well, he had never known or dreamed of anything like it, 'and you never did either,' he jibed at the envious ones.

After that it got to be a habit, with no questions asked. Sometimes, especially if he had a busy schedule, it was just a grab and a wrestle, in-again-out-again-Finnegan and good-by. Other days they would talk and get to know each other. You couldn't tell about her. Every so often she liked to be quiet. She would just lie there babbling about this and that, and no matter how he tried to capture her attention she would ramble on.

It was a dewy, breezy May morning, the morning of the fifteenth. The exterminator strolled up the front walk whistling 'Yankee Doodle' and grinning at the thought that he too would be going to town, in his fashion, as soon as he got rid of the upstairs roaches. He stuck his head in the doorway, crying, as usual: 'Exterminator!' Hearing her answer from somewhere inside, he went up to the top floor. The can up there was in bad shape. Roaches were running all over the place. He shook his head disgustedly, and his eyes gleamed behind the horn-rimmed spectacles. He went down on one knee like a machine gunner, firing streams of musky liquid into all corners. Clouds of spray filled the bathroom. The roaches keeled over one after another until not one could be seen moving. 'There!' he murmured, and with a pleased glance at the linoleum battlefield he went down to the next landing.

On the stairway he encountered a young tenant whose face was familiar. 'Hey, have the roaches been much trouble this month?' he asked.

'That's a coincidence,' answered the young fellow, who was lugging a pair of heavy suitcases. 'I was just noticing that there weren't so many around this month. You must have done a pretty good job.'

'Oh, I don't know,' said the exterminator, and by way of showing his thanks he inquired: 'Leaving?'

The young fellow nodded. 'That's right, I'm pulling up stakes.'

'Need any help?'

The boy thanked him; no, he didn't. He struggled off downstairs with the suitcases bumping his heels, and the exterminator continued on his rounds.

'Feeling pretty good today,' he murmured to himself. He felt kind of like a rough-and-tumble, but when she opened the door he recognized the mild, distracted look on her pink face, and knew that it would have to be a quiet one.

'What's the trouble, baby?' he asked, while he carefully squirted around the sink.

She fell back into her rocking-chair, fanning herself with a damp towel. It was something she did a great deal of the time, for the kitchen was humid to the point of fogginess, and ventilated like a small stockyard.

'Did you see him?' she gasped. 'He's leaving, he really is!'

The exterminator approached her, breathing hard.

'Who's leaving, baby? What's the difference? Come on, I never felt so good, I – '

She fended him off, going on in the same tone of absent-minded distress: 'I don't see what got into him. He says he's got to move to the Circle Hotel. I asked him why, and he says: "Oh, it's nearer the center of things." Why does he have to be in the center? Where does he think he's going to get the money to stay at a hotel like that? I thought, maybe I hurt his feelings – '

'Oh, my Jesus!' the exterminator interrupted with an anguished whisper. He had taken hold of one pulpy arm, and such was his condition and the tropical atmosphere of the kitchen that the flesh in his hand drove him almost out of his mind.

'Well, I saw him,' he said desperately, without much sense, 'he's all right. Don't worry about him. I tell you, he's a good kid. So what if he's leaving? You can get twenty guys by tomorrow, so will you *please* – '

She allowed him to haul her into the parlor, but even as he began kissing her she went on plaintively: 'I didn't mean to scare him about raising the rent. He shouldn't have taken it so seriously. "Goodness knows," I said, "that's all right, Mr Hingham, just forget I ever mentioned it." But no, he says, without any resentfulness at all, he's got to leave for business reasons. He didn't seem to be mad or anything, but he was funny. For instance, he was smoking a cigarette, and he never used to. You know, he was always such a nice boy; you could be sure there wasn't any harm in him. This morning, though, the way he looked at me . . . I mean, he was still shy, but with a boldness too, as if he was sweet sixteen but if he had the chance – Ooh! What are you trying to do, sweetie, break my back?'

'Oh lord, baby, be with me!' the exterminator cried, with his sallow face screwed into a kind of agony and his glasses falling down to his nostrils. 'Talk to me, be with me!'

'Make me know it, baby,' she replied dutifully, eluding his frantic mouth, then explaining to the wall: 'It's not the money I lose until the next one moves in . . . but he was such a well-appearing, well-spoken . . . oh . . . I was getting to know . . . and who'll I get now – a firebug maybe, some crook.'

With what seemed to be his last breath the exterminator groaned: 'Oh, christly!'

'What I mean is, it's not nice for people to say about my house that a fellow would leave when rooms are hard to get. It's like an insult . . . What's the matter, honey, are you mad with me?'

She patted her lover on his pointed, thatched-roof head. She searched the length of him with motherly concern and would have closed him in her arms. But he pushed her rudely on the chin, stood up, and began straightening his clothes.

'Oh, lovely! I'm sorry, it's just that I was worrying.'

The exterminator continued sullenly to avoid her eyes. 'Just like a woman,' he snarled. Reaching for his cockroach gun, he started for the door. She rose from the couch and rolled toward him, her arms outflung, in massive uncorseted disorder.

'You'll be coming back, won't you?' she begged.

'Well, I don't know,' said the exterminator in an injured tone. 'I don't know as I'm welcome.'

At this she fell on his shoulders, beseeching his forgiveness. The next time things would be different.

'All right,' the exterminator agreed after a while. He had to be getting on, and her embraces were already having an effect on him.

Outside he heaved a long sigh. He felt sort of small and foolish; that was the trouble after being with her. He climbed into his truck and raced the motor. 'Well,' he thought, not for the first time, 'you can't be fussy.' Then, pounding a triumphant honk on his horn, he drove away.

9

In the Center

The telephone kept ringing, and Hal wished someone would answer it. He pulled the pillow around his head. He had dreamed that he was in the middle of a jostling crowd, and suddenly the people turned, smiling, and tipped their hats. The room seemed to grow lighter, and he made out the telephone just beyond his hand. Soft alarms were vibrating the little bed table.

'Mr Hingham . . .'

'Yes. I am.'

'It's eight o'clock, sir.'

'Who?' he said. 'Eight. Well, thank you.'

He lay back peacefully, and as the room took shape so did his new life that had brought him here. In the weak morning light he saw the fragments of himself, hotel guest. His suitcases lay open and empty on the rug where he had left them yesterday, before starting on the Walk. His suits seemed a row of Hal Hinghams in the closet, primly right-faced, as if waiting to reach for a necktie and march away in the shiny shoes arranged below them.

The morning was gray. Gusts smote the wet window-panes. He felt the shaking of the wind, and something clanked outside his window. He didn't mind. He liked it here at the Circle Hotel. His muscles ached from yesterday's exercise. He could remember hardly anything of the Walk – not that this mattered. His experiences were stored away in his unconscious mind, and would automatically give him the right answers when the time came to centralize someone.

The idea occurred to him: 'Everybody's getting up now.' He shaved and showered, and the bathroom echoed with his tuneless whistling. Presently he stood in the middle of the room in his neat gabardine and topcoat, wearing the soft brown hat slanted down over his brow. He had a vague feeling of having lost something, and searched his pockets. It couldn't be important, he decided, and went downstairs.

The desk clerk with the nervous stomach beamed at him. 'How did it go last night, sir?'

'Fine!' Hal called back, still not knowing what he was going to say until, marvelously, it was on his tongue: 'That hot-milk idea of yours did the trick!' He crossed the lobby. In a succession of long mirrors he saw the clerk bemused in admiration of himself.

Outside, in the raw weather, he started for his office. As he walked up Boyleston Street, the wind lessened. In the distance, the towers of the Arcadia Life building reminded him of his safe and modest place in the scheme of things. He was on his way to ask Fred Purdy's permission to Take A Business Trip. On this trip he would Make Good. But before leaving town, at his age, he would get engaged tonight to the Sweetest Girl In The World. 'How easy it all is when you just do what you're supposed to do,' he thought happily.

He told Fred Purdy that he wanted to try his luck in Bradford and Riverton, the territory where his dad had got started.

'Outdo the old man?' he laughed. 'No, I'm only going to make a little splash. Your fellows down there won't notice me.'

'Why the sudden ambition?' asked the agency-director. He was thinking that it would be a relief not to see Hingham's wounded personality every morning.

'It's your doing, Mr Purdy – the last time we talked. You've made me realize that life is a complete waste of time, but I might as well waste it profitably, don't you think?'

'All right, go ahead,' said Purdy absently.

'It's wonderful not to believe in anything,' said Hingham, getting up. 'As you say, unbelief frees a man for action. I want to thank you.'

'What?'

'I'll be gone for a couple of weeks. I hope the company will have faith in me – for laughs, of course.'

'Hey, what's happened to you?' Fred Purdy cried in delight. He had always wanted a son to join him in making fun of the world.

But Hingham was already on his way.

* * *

After lunch Hal went back to his hotel room with three boxes containing blank insurance policies. He put these in one suitcase, and packed the other with his nylon traveling clothes. Then, having nothing to do until his date with Rose, he sat down with the *Revelations*. One passage had been bothering him – the WORK CENTRALLY commandment. He read:

Despite your power to make anyone do your bidding, you should not rise to the top. Get ahead, but moderately. Work at a typical job for an ordinary salary . . .

It didn't seem right. A Centralist had no way of insuring his future. Somewhere along the line (Dr Modesto didn't mention this) it was perfectly possible that he might wake up one morning to find that he had lost his Centralistic powers. Without his protective magic, he would once again be helpless before the contempt and indifference of the world. But if he had *money* this couldn't happen. All he asked was a bit of security . . .

It was wrong to doubt Dr Modesto. He drove the destructive little thoughts out of his mind, and forced his attention on something else – his evening with Rose. He was dressing for the most important date of his life. This time, for once, he wouldn't be afraid of running into her roommate and the football-player. He actually hoped that Gladys and Heffernan would be there. He would amaze them. In the past he had been paralyzed by their heavy humor. He had cowered in the corner and desperately read magazines while they horsed around the living-room. But tonight he would know how to horse and banter with Gladys, and win Heffernan's respect with uncouth remarks.

10
Spring Practice

The golden-haired girl moved along the sideline. They had just turned the floodlights on. The lamps glared through the drizzle, giving the ground a frosty look, although it was far too warm for football on the last day of spring practice.

'RUN IT AGAIN. JUST EASY NOW!' a voice roared from somewhere out of the floodlights. The command echoed around the empty stadium. The speaker was resting on one knee under an umbrella. His coat sleeve brushed the hand microphone and the atmosphere crackled. He was surrounded by several other umbrellas under which his assistants and half a dozen sportswriters huddled and made notes.

The girl looked nine feet tall as she walked away from them. Her transparent raincoat blazed as if lighted from within. She seemed a hardy apparition stalking the field, impatient for the best player to come and claim her.

'RUN!'

The quarterback bent over behind the center, calling signals. The opposing lines crouched in the mud, but when the ball was snapped they moved gently against one another – with the exception of the defensive left tackle. He went slaughtering through token resistance, and as the little quarterback ran wide behind his blockers the entire backfield was suddenly piled up and smashed back onto the ball-carrier. They all went down in a stunned heap near the sideline where the girl stopped pacing and examined them with cold distaste.

'JUDAS PRIEST, HEFFERNAN! I SAID TAKE IT EASY!' The voice out of the amplifier filled the sky.

A figure carrying a black bag ran out on the field.

'What was the idea of that, Heffernan!'

But the tackle ignored the frantic voices. He was pursuing the tall blonde in the bright raincoat down the sideline. She ran easily, but in no hurry. He caught her by the boards and after a brief struggle, plastered a kiss on her. Then he came loping back, occasionally leaping in great hurdles through the air.

'A big kid,' muttered a sportswriter disgustedly.

'So he's going to be All-America – does he have a license – '

'They give that Heffernan too much latitude. It'll catch up with 'em, bringing his girl to practice. Look at her!' another said.

She had returned, and as coolly as before watched the doctor get the shattered backfield on its feet. 'They're all going to live, coach!' he called out.

'OKAY, LET'S RUN IT OVER AGAIN.'

In the stands, a bantam, bleak-faced spectator helplessly followed the girl's every move and brooded on his distorted sexuality. Jack Swan handled public relations for the team. It was one of his lesser accounts – not to be compared, for example, with a client like Arcadia Life – but he was paying entirely too much attention to the Bay State U. Athletic Association. He knew why. It was the chance of seeing her. He crouched under his dripping hat and thought about himself. Thirty-five and married, he was infatuated with this great creature who belonged to a football-player.

He hadn't so much as kissed her, yet he couldn't get Gladys out of his mind. He hung about in the wings, sick with lust. She was ruining him. He concentrated more on her than on his job. Worse, when he did see her she made him act like a fool.

His chance came during the uproar over Heffernan. He quickly went down to the sideline and approached her in the obsequious manner he was helpless to control.

'How that guy of yours can hit!'

'Yes,' she replied, unmoved, looking down on him as she always did, making a point of it. 'Are you ready for tonight like we agreed?'

He wondered whether she had any idea what he really thought of Heffernan. 'Sure, Gladys. You want me to really pitch, as if I – '

'I want to get Rose away from this Hingham creep. We'll take her to the party and introduce her around. You just show her a good time, but no passes,' she reminded him sternly. 'I know, beautiful.' He dared to pat her. 'What's the program?'

'We'll meet Johnny at the Growler. Then I have to go home and sort of tell her gradually. You two can wait and have a few.' Unexpectedly she favored him with a smile. 'Remember the last time he broke training?'

'Yes,' he said.

Seeing that Heffernan was about to come off the field, he returned to his place in the stands.

Later, in the Growler, while they waited for Johnny Heffernan, Swan suspected that he would have been better off missing the big drunk. It could be a nasty evening, he thought, with Heffernan loaded, and this roommate he was supposed to kid along but not lay his hands on . . . He had heard of the roommate. A dud. Still, he would have to do his best. He looked at Gladys out of the corner of his eye, and a small thrill went through him. He would hate to cross her!

The hot beer hall gave him a flushed and sensual feeling. At the other tables the college boys were already chug-a-lugging, and mauling their dates. Gladys's big white shoulder excited him. She must have noticed it, for she put her arm against his, rocking him a little, and he felt her careless affection and contempt.

He knew his position was in a small way humiliating. Perhaps he ought to try acting superior to her – as if anyone could, he thought with odd satisfaction. He imagined her at the hospital, where she was a nurse. She marched through the wards, no doubt, her voice carrying everywhere. She was really stupid, he thought with sudden vindictiveness. Her arrogance was founded on stupidity. Or was it all physical? Because she was so big?

He liked her style. She strode about in a manner that said nobody ever violated this girl. But she had been, many times. He could imagine how often Heffernan put the boots to her.

Gladys yawned and drained her glass of beer, and he cried: 'Waiter! Waiter! Two more!'

He remembered the last time, the last drunk at her place when Heffernan got to the point he always did, of wanting to wrestle. (She had sent the roommate off somewhere.) His stunt was to wrestle three men at once, and he did, and threw everybody over the couches. And suddenly he had turned to her, saying: 'I'm ready, baby!' When everybody saw the way they looked at each other, the whole crowd ran for the door. For a moment, in the corridor, he'd had a sneaking desire to go back and watch or at least listen. But he was never even to glimpse her, he knew, except the way he did now.

'Here he comes,' she was saying, 'move over,' and her command was his wish.

Heffernan came in, and a few cheers went up. The college boys reached out to shake hands, or just touch him. He was picking his nose and looked at nobody. He had a placid, almost sleepy mien – unless he was playing football or drunk. He sat down without saying anything. Swan twisted around avidly, watching Gladys regard her man with growing pleasure.

'You're already out of shape, you big tank,' she said.

The tackle chewed gum steadily. 'You think so?' he said. He rolled up his shirt. 'Go ahead.'

The girl laughed and struck him hard near the belt line, causing him to wince.

'Wise apple,' he said. 'You hit low.'

Swan laughed meanly: 'Some punch,' and wished he hadn't, because Heffernan immediately got red. He laughed hurriedly as the football-player grabbed his glass of beer. 'Take it, Johnny! I've got a head start on you.'

The football-player pushed his thumb in Swan's direction. 'What's Shrimpo here for?' he asked Gladys.

'I brought him for Rose, honey. It's all right with you, isn't it? He's just the right size for her too,' she added, nudging Swan with her shoulder.

He sat there meekly, after having his hair tousled, but his pride was hurt at last, and he asked himself: 'What am I doing here with this pair of animals? I am their superior in every way, except the physical.' At moments he hated her. She was bold and yet bovine, as Heffernan was placid and bovine. They were bull and cow to his – what? Rabbit. 'But I'm a man,' thought Swan, 'an educated man. I should be able to rise above my perversions.'

'You don't mind if he and Rose come along, do you, honey?' asked Gladys, clasping the football-player's hand.

Heffernan popped his gum. 'I don't mind anybody,' he said finally, 'so long as they don't get wise.' He stood up and announced: 'I'm gonna get a couple of bottles.' Conceit gave his face a peaceful look. Swan glanced enviously at the apish arms that Gladys adored.

'He gets all his liquor from his father's store,' Gladys said admiringly, after the football-player had gone. She turned to her undersized companion. 'Now listen,' she said. 'The idea is, you give Rose a good time, but no funny business. Remember, she's an innocent kid.'

'Well, so am I,' began Swan facetiously, until he saw that she was serious. At such moments her eyes bulged and she pondered loudly over the most trivial matters. 'Why does her stupidity excite me?' he asked himself. He was always searching for clues to himself, and this seemed a promising lead. But it was too easy: 'It's because I want her to misunderstand – and hurt me.'

'Now listen,' she repeated, unaware of his small start of devotion. 'Rose is a funny little kid. The trouble is, she's not confident of herself. She's scared of everybody, except this creep she goes with. But she's worth a lot better, if she'd only get out of herself! So that's what you've got to do – make her feel like a woman, in a nice way.'

'A nice way? What's that?' He knew that his laughter was foolish.

'*You know what I mean.*'

'Oh, yes,' he agreed quickly. He was grateful to her; in an animal way she understood him. 'She's really kind,' he thought, as she warned him: 'You be good!'

11

Waiting for an Undistinguished Lover

A pale shadowless evening was falling on the streets outside her window. Rose wondered whether it was going to rain. There was a smell of salt in the air. The streetlights were misty. For safety's sake she would take her raincoat, although he might then suggest walking in the rain for fun and exercise.

She moved closer to the window and watched the couples strolling in the dusk. She waited without interest for his coming. She didn't mind waiting. It was when he arrived, seeing him, talking to him, that she felt lonely. She felt isolated when she walked with him. The timid boy friend who took her away from the rest of the world did not even want her for himself.

She was nearly twenty-six. It was time, as Gladys said, to give him an ultimatum. The certain outcome of this crisis made Rose clench her hands and long to slap the meek, stubborn smile she knew would appear on Hal's face at the mention of marriage. But she couldn't slap away his weakness. Whatever drastic threat she made he would accept as one more misfortune, shrug his shoulders hopelessly, and disappear from her life as quietly and timidly as he had entered it.

The door slammed and Gladys burst into the bedroom. 'Rose, come on. We're going out on a date.'

'What?' Rose said. 'What date?'

'I've got a fellow who wants to meet you. He's coming over with Johnny.'

'Who? Oh, no, I can't! Coming over *here*?'

'In a half-hour. So you hurry – '

'Gladys, I can't. Hal's going to be – '

'Him,' Gladys laughed. 'What difference does he make?'

She had already undressed and flung herself on the bed. Encountering her severe blue eyes, Rose turned away and caught a glimpse of herself in the mirror. She had never been more unattractive. The little red bowler was still askew. It would not sit properly. It perched on the very top of her head, tilted, or slid too far to one side. No matter how she fixed it, the hat looked as if she had dropped it on at the last moment.

'I'm not going out with you,' she said in a shrill voice.

'Why not? Didn't you say last night you ought to get rid of him?'

It was true.

'Well, this is the way to do it. All at once. Tell him you're sorry but something else has come up.'

'Please . . .' Rose began. All she could think of was that they would soon be at the door, then sitting in the living-room, and Hal might walk in on them. 'It isn't right without any warning. Say I'll come with you next week,' she pleaded.

'No,' Gladys said. She was performing a languid exercise, arching her back. 'I know you. You'd have another excuse.' She got up and gave Rose a hug. 'Don't worry. This fellow is very nice – and I'll be watching over you.'

As she went into the bathroom, she called back over her shoulder: 'You'll thank me, honey!'

The water plunged in the bathtub. Gladys was singing.

Rose crouched forward with her elbows on the dressing-table, peering desperately into the mirror. She pulled the hat this way and that. It seemed to come alive as though animated by a jealous witch, clawing her hair and catching on the point of a loose hairpin.

'I'm making it worse,' she thought, which was true. The hat wasn't the only thing wrong now. Her struggle with it had set a progressive ugliness in motion, beginning with her mouth. Her lips pressed into a thin line. Tendons stood out in her neck, deepening the hollows there, bringing out the collar bones – accentuating the impression of meagerness that she needed, above all else, to conceal. It was too bad. Her complexion appeared to have taken on the hue of tin. She squinted and frowned, deteriorating further. The sight of her sharp elbows emerging from the short-sleeved green blouse drove away the last remnants of her self-confidence. 'How ugly I am!' she cried to herself, and the doorbell rang.

'Gladys!'

There was no answer but a thrashing in the tub.

'They're here!'

'Well, let them in, Rose!'

'No, I can't. I don't want to see them.' She opened the bathroom door, and was hardly able to breathe for the steam. 'You've got to tell them to go away.'

'Answer the door! What's the matter?' demanded Gladys.

The bell rang over and over again under the pressure of a heavy thumb.

'They might see him!' said Rose, in a panic.

'God!' exclaimed Gladys. She threw on a bathrobe and ran dripping to the front door. There was a stamping and commotion in the hallway.

'That football-player,' thought Rose in despair. When Gladys came back she clasped her imploringly. 'Please get them out of here, just for a little while, until after I leave with Hal.'

'You see. That shows what you think of him. You're ashamed of him.'

'I'm afraid – '

'I wouldn't think of going with a man my friends didn't respect.'

Sounds of coarse hilarity came from the living-room, and Rose knew that Johnny Heffernan must be getting drunk. A mean little laugh followed his guffaw. Her date!

She ran to the bed and threw herself down, in tears. Gladys was talking to her soothingly, but she wouldn't answer. She kept whispering: 'Please, tell them . . .' until Gladys went away. She heard her go into the other room and say something. There were more commotions, protests, and swearing, but presently all was quiet. Rose rested with her head in her arms, exhausted. Gladys went back into the bathroom.

After a while she came out, and Rose lifted her head.

'Gladys, thank you.'

Gladys bent over and kissed her. 'She thinks I'm sick,' Rose thought. 'Maybe I am.' 'Did they go?' she asked timidly.

'They sure did, honey.'

Rose sat up. 'I'm sorry.' Tears had brightened her green eyes, and as she struggled to smile she became rather charming. 'You see, I was afraid – your friends wouldn't like me very much.'

She didn't add that she had never liked the kind of men Gladys went with. Her roommate traveled with a loud bunch. They were good-looking, as a rule, and well dressed, and had money. But they were bold and rough. They talked in a brutal manner, which changed to a silly bantering tone when they spoke to 'females.' They were also free with their hands. (She couldn't stand this; her elbows would fly up.) She shivered at the idea of being married to one of these. Yet all the men she had ever been with acted in much the same way – except Hal, who refused to be a man.

She had met him at a dance given by the alumni of the Browning & Snow School of Business Administration. The fellow who brought her had got drunk in the men's room. She had turned for help to the nearest boy, Hal, who was standing alone watching the dancers. She explained her predicament and he was sympathetic. He even made an ineffectual attempt to revive the boy in the men's room.

'Might as well take you home, I guess.'

Hal's lack of aggressiveness had been refreshing then. It had seemed cute three years ago. When they walked across the Common in the moonlight she had been ready for him to get fresh, but it didn't enter his head.

'Well, good night.'

In the end it was she who gave him a dry puckering kiss and ran into the house.

'Rose, you're not wearing *that*,' said Gladys.

Before she could protest, the bowler was whisked from her head.

'Honey, it's not your style.' Gladys took Rose's brush and comb, and commanded: 'You sit still now.'

In a minute she had all the pins out. Gladys brushed her hair in long smooth strokes, each one ending in a comforting tug, as if to signify: 'Now that's done, and that one, and that one.' The rhythmic stroking made Rose sleepy. 'I wish we could stay home by ourselves,' she thought.

'Rose, you've got to hold your head up!'

She changed her position, but in doing so put herself in a bad light. Again her compelexion had the tin hue. She had wondered, but never dared ask Dr Warren, whether X-ray work might affect her health. Of course she stayed out of the room while the picture was being snapped, but the secondary radiation that remained could do something to a technician over a period of years.

'Now you're pretty,' said Gladys, stepping back. 'Look at yourself.'

She was. Her hair fell in soft black waves. Her image in the glass appeared softer and more feminine.

'Why don't you change your mind now? Come out with us.'

'No. Maybe some day.'

'All right,' Gladys said. 'I'm going to tell you – and, believe me, I know – there's something wrong with you. You need to talk to a psychiatrist.'

'I guess I do,' Rose answered feebly.

'Otherwise you wouldn't be hanging on to a fellow who doesn't satisfy you in any way. He doesn't even want to marry you. Look, honey, you're getting older.'

'I know it!'

'But you're afraid of men. You're sticking with this one *because* he never makes a pass, *because* he doesn't treat you like a woman. Something in your past makes you – look, I'm serious. I can get you one of the psychiatrists at the hospital.'

'Yes, it's probably a good idea,' said Rose in a small, choked voice.

The doorbell sounded, and she ran with teetering little steps to answer it.

Gladys admired herself in black slacks and a black-and-white striped blouse. She reminded herself of a lion-tamer. But she had to admit exultantly that her guy was one who could not be tamed. On this night of the big drunk, when the big guy would break training, she felt the approaching climax of the season.

They had saved up for it. The only problem was to get the football-player home in shape. For this, Swan would be along to help. She paced about the room with growing excitement. She thought of Heffernan's slab of a torso, and wild plans began to develop in her mind. They were interrupted by a scream from the living-room and Rose's frightened cry: 'Hal! What are you doing!'

Gladys bounded to the door. She heard Hal laugh. 'That's right, they're for you.'

There was Rose standing in a bad light, an astonished little creature whose neck tendons quivered and showed too plainly, holding a long box in which three orchids nestled in green tissue paper.

'Get your coat on,' said her boy friend, chuckling. 'We're going to Childs' Old France.'

12

The Love-Date

'Childs' Old France,' Hal told the taxi-driver. 'Make it snappy.' He completely dominated the taxi-driver. Once he warned him: 'Watch out! Got valuable property in here,' he said. 'The girl I'm going to marry.'

'Marry!' said the taxi-driver. 'So that's the story!'

'Yes,' he said. 'So watch out, watch out. This is my girl.'

Hal took her in his arms and kissed her. Girls like spontaneity. It makes them think they have driven a fellow out of his pattern. With careful spontaneity he kissed her again.

They were caught in traffic, and held hands in the gloomy, vibrating cab. The meter ticked, the numbers jumped. They only had eyes for each other. He observed her luminous little face in the light of a cut-rate drugstore. What he saw in her eyes astonished him. He tightened his grasp on her hands, as if to protect himself from the hungry little animal he had created.

In order to centralize himself to her he gazed at the drugstore window, and went momentarily to sleep among the hoses, home permanents, and syringes. He filled his mind with enormous price tags. As the cab began to move, he found the mood he wanted, and turned to her knowingly – and they were at each other's throats, nuzzling and kissing. Before fixing his lips on hers he said: 'You don't know how I love you.'

At Childs' he argued with the waiters. He was a smooth loudmouth. 'Not that table on the aisle,' he told them. 'In the corner. That's for us. That's all we want. That's all we'll take.' They took the RESERVED sign off in a hurry.

When she came back from powdering her nose, he had already ordered her a very dry martini. She watched him order – as if he were an habitué of Childs' – two old-fashioneds for him, two martinis for her; shrimp cocktails, soup de jour, lobsters with drawn butter and fingerbowls, and coffee.

The drinks made her dizzy, and all at once she collapsed before his charm. She swayed and groped toward him. His face had a strange bland beauty that destroyed all her inhibitions. She kept reaching for him, and she knew she was mouthing confessions and confidences to his smiling face. After a while she was laughing hysterically because she couldn't eat any of the lovely things he had ordered. Her hunger was only for him. He smiled wisely and ordered coffee, repeating at intervals, with a tenderness she could not possibly deserve from any man: 'You don't know, Rose. You just don't know!'

The band played, and they did a wobbly dance. He requested a rumba, and they played it. He held himself hard against her as they moved from the hips, somehow knowing how to do it, hugging one another, swaying and falling. Two drunken children in love.

The dancing and coffee sobered her. But before she could get her bearings they were off again. They went to one spot after another, in more taxis.

In the Sphinx Club it happened. A delicate boy was playing negligently on a little piano. She realized that he was getting really serious. 'I've got big ambitions now!' he whispered, as the piano-player came down hard on some blue chords. 'I'd like to ask a certain somebody if she'd share them with me.'

She almost fainted. His dry hands clutched her shoulders. She threw her arms around his neck and hung on him.

'I love you, Hal.'

'You know what?' he said. 'I love you also. Let's go to your house.'

'I can lick any lousy Harvard bastid in this place.'

'I'm sure you can, old man. Now would you mind leaving us alone?'

'I'll leave you on your ass, 'n' every faaken Harvard – '

'Come on, Johnny, Gladys said – '

'I can whip everybody's ass.'

'Sure, you can, but – '

'Who *is* this meatball?'

'Johnny, she's waiting in the car. Remember, she warned you.'

'What'd he call me?'

'Who? I don't know. Never mind.'

'That wise apple over there. I'm gonna belt him!'

76

'But Gladys told you – '
'Faakah!'

Gladys heard the familiar tinkle and crash of glass, and Swan came running out of the bar across the street. She honked the horn and he ran to her.

'Johnny's in trouble!' he panted. 'I told him what you said, but he wouldn't listen. The police are coming!'

'Get in,' she said, moving behind the wheel.

Swan jumped in beside her. He was shivering. 'Shouldn't we help him?' he said. 'I mean . . .' he appealed to her. 'Shouldn't a man try – '

'He doesn't need any help,' she said. She noticed for the first time that Swan had eyes like a little bug. He was cute.

'What's the use of trying to help the big moron? He's going to drink and fight until he passes out,' she said bitterly.

A chair flew out of the bright doorway across the street, followed by a man who collapsed on the sidewalk. The din increased, and they heard yells and Johnny Heffernan's bellow from within.

Swan suddenly felt himself seized about the waist. A great determined mouth descended on his, and his senses reeled.

'You've waited a long time, Buster,' he heard her say, 'let's go do it.'

He stared at her in terror. It was all very well to dream, but . . . 'No!' he cried, breaking out of her arms. 'I'm going back in there to help my friend!'

He leaped out of the car. She saw him run madly for the doorway, and disappear into the melee just as the police car pulled up to the curb.

It was nearly daylight before she and Swan managed to bail out the football-player and lug him home. They arrived at the door of the frat house, and she could go no farther.

'I'll get him upstairs – somehow,' Swan gasped. 'Got to – patch him up.' This was obviously a lie, because Heffernan's fists were the only bruised part of him, and the blood spattered over his clothes was that of other people. But he was sodden drunk. 'Got to see – bones broken – ' Swan insisted. He resembled a desperate rabbit in the dawn light. He hadn't dared to look at her since the fiasco in the car.

'Take him,' she said. 'I'm sure you boys will get to know each other better.'

She let go her share of the slumbering football-player, who toppled out of Swan's arms and lay spread-eagled in a bed of nasturtiums.

Swan gazed after her as she marched to the car. 'God,' he thought, 'I've been a failure tonight.'

Snores came from the open windows of the frat house.

Gladys found all the lights in the apartment burning. She hurried into the bedroom. Rose was asleep with her clothes on. Gladys went quietly to the bed, and stopped in amazement.

Rose looked as if she had been badly injured, but she was smiling. Her mouth and cheeks were bruised. Her hair was wanton. She seemed almost depraved, with her disordered hair, the blouse torn several inches down the left shoulder, and the rainbow skirt rumpled and tossed halfway up her thighs.

Gladys was shocked. 'Like a little animal,' she thought, and whispered loudly: 'Rose!'

Her roommate stirred and groaned sensually.

'Rose!'

She became aware that the sleeper's eyes had opened. Rose was looking at her with a mysterious and knowing smile.

'What is it, honey?' Gladys cried. 'What happened?'

Slowly, Rose lowered her eyes.

'Well, look at her! You little . . .' Gladys exclaimed, cradling Rose in her arms. She had meant to take a joking tone, but something in Rose's manner made her nervous.

'You *did*?'

She was actually relieved when Rose burst into tears, and comforted her with rough affection. 'Never mind. It isn't much fun the first time, is it?'

'Yes!'

'What?' said Gladys, drawing back. 'Then what are you crying for?'

'I don't know.'

'*Tell* me.'

'Hal wanted to come back here,' Rose said, 'and – you know . . .'

'Here,' said Gladys, 'in this room?'

Rose nodded.

'Suppose we might have come in.'

'I guess we should have thought of that,' answered Rose softly, without interest.

Gladys regarded her with growing perplexity and annoyance. 'I must say you don't look very attractive.'

'I know,' said Rose, sitting up. 'I'm an awful mess. And my head aches. Do we have any aspirin?'

'Yes,' Gladys said.

She watched Rose limp into the bathroom. As she waited slumped on the bed, she felt big and ugly. She noticed specks of some Harvard man's blood on her blouse.

'I suppose you'll be seeing each other all the time now.'

'Not for a while! He's going away to Bradford and then to Riverton, and then he'll come back and we'll get married.'

A gentle gargling came from the bathroom. Gray morning light invaded the ravaged bedroom. Gladys got up heavily and looked for a cigarette. She could find only butts.

13
The Centralist's Walk

It was nine o'clock in the morning in Bradford, Massachusetts, now a manufacturing city, once the world's greatest whaling port. A businesslike young man wearing a slanted hat trotted down the steps of the Hotel Leviathan.

Hal Hingham walked briskly down Prospect Street. His eyes were clear and bright and glassy. So was his mind. His face was emptied of all expression. He would have resembled an amnesia victim, except that when people approached from the other direction he seemed to waken – as if in response to an electric beam – and he gave back the same signs of life they showed to him.

He exchanged friendly glances with two members of the Bradford Junior Chamber of Commerce. One Jaycee asked: 'Isn't he one of our bunch? I could have sworn . . .' Meanwhile the object of their attention had become an entirely different person. He dragged himself exhaustedly past a knocked-out garage mechanic who was shambling home after the night shift. A few seconds later he was whistling along with a sailor. He blessed somebody in a turned-around collar. A vacuous housemaid drew a blank. At nine thirty he reached the corner of Pike and Scupper streets, the center of Bradford, and started on his tour of the town.

Toward the third hour someone whom Hal didn't see began following him. He was a tall, thin boy of graduate-student age. He needed a haircut. When he stood still, he looked like a weed that had grown up through a crack in the sidewalk.

Hal came out of a supermarket and waited for a traffic light to change. A few years away, the boy was regarding him furiously and scribbling things on a clip board. His brow was screwed into a tortured question mark. Together the Centralist and his pursuer moved through the streets. The day wore on. They shopped through a department store. The face peered after Hal, even into the men's room. Later the thin hand grasped a strap at the other end of the trolley he was riding, while its owner performed gymnastics to hide the hieroglyphics he entered on some kind of record sheet.

Hal sensed the recurring shadow following him. He heard a cough behind him. He saw the boy lurking behind a barber's pole, in frantic secrecy trying to impress notes on a flapping sheet of paper. Turning quickly, he approached the person who was shadowing him. The boy drew away, startled and confused.

The weedy boy carried a cup of coffee in one hand and his clip board in the other. He pressed a thickness of question-and-answer forms to his heart. The top sheet bore the legend SLOTTON SURVEY. He had forgotten to remove a pencil from behind his ear. His necktie hung askew and his seersucker jacket was stained across the shoulders. Something worried him. He frowned at the maze of diners in the middle of the restaurant. Keeping his eye on this area, he went over to a table near the wall.

'Hi, Randy!'

The man at the table also had a clip board. He was gloomily eating a doughnut and didn't look up to see who had addressed him.

'Time out for tea, eh?'

The man raised his head, which was dark and heavy, and said: 'Hello, Duncan. No, as a matter of fact I'm having coffee.'

'Oh, please don't make a fool of me,' the boy appealed. 'Listen, there's something I've got to talk to you about. It's happening right now, but don't look!'

He stood up and gazed across the cafeteria.

'What the hell is wrong with you, Duncan?'

'It's okay. He's still there, with his back to us. Randy, there's a strange one walking the streets today. He's like a wild atom.'

The dark man sighed and lit a cigarette.

Duncan thrust his shining eyes, nose, and forehead across the table. 'You know what Dr Slotton wants us to do, beginning next week. *Follow one person*,' he whispered. 'For horizontal observation, you know, in addition to the sampling. Well, I thought I'd get in some practice. So I tried it out today. Look. See that fellow over there, in the middle of them all? The one with the slanted hat?'

'Uh.'

'He's the one I picked out to follow. He looked sort of typical, as you can see.'

'I don't see him.'

'That's just it!' said the boy. 'He'd be right in front of me, and then he'd vanish. I kept losing him. The thing is, he's *more there* than anyone else, and that's why you don't notice him.'

His colleague cursed as he accidentally dropped his cigarette into his coffee cup. 'What are you talking about?' he said in a disgusted tone.

'I'm worried about this fellow. I logged his routine, but he doesn't have any routine.'

'That's his affair, I would think.'

'Sure. Of course, it's ours too – if the Slotton Survey is following him. But this guy who doesn't seem to be going anywhere sort of *imitates* the other people on the street. Secretly, one by one, as they come along. Nobody notices it. He just – '

'A nut, obviously.'

'No, he isn't. For instance, he pleases everybody. But they don't know it. They unconsciously smile and hang around him in patterns as he walks. Randy, I think he's from some rival outfit.'

'Could be.'

'The reason I think so . . .' The boy shivered. 'He caught me finally. He turned around and asked me my occupation.'

'I didn't – I couldn't.' Duncan blushed. 'I told him it was confidential.'

'Hah, hah, hah!' roared the dark man. 'Hah, hah, hah, hah, hah!'

'All right,' said the boy. He sipped at his coffee. In spite of his humiliation, he didn't forget to make sure that the slanted hat was still in the cafeteria. 'You laugh, but I believe in Dr Slotton. I believe in Science. I believe in the Complete Predictability of mankind. What's a human being? From birth to death, he's a constantly changing set of statistics with arms and legs – '

'Bull, Duncan.'

'You can never escape being a statistic, even in the most private moments. Even, we know, in the act of love. Take a person. Who is that walking down the street? You say Smith. I say he's rural to urban, occasional glass of beer, believes in vitamins, woman's place is in the home, and so on, until after you've criss-crossed him enough, Smith, as such, vanishes.'

'Everybody's vanishing on you today.'

'Laugh.' Duncan waved his arms at the ponderous face opposite him. 'That's the only way we'll ever get to understand humanity.'

He brooded. 'I can't get this fellow with the slanted hat out of my mind. If Dr Slotton knows what he's doing, this fellow has got to be using the *wrong methods*. The way he walks around, with those imitations nobody can see! Everywhere, for hours, in and out of buildings, in the stores, through the park. All he does is walk, and they don't notice him especially, but they form patterns around him just the same. Walk, walk, walk, but no sampling at all. This is science? He's like the Pied Piper or something. He's figured this town out. I know he has, but I haven't got valid proof. Unless I ask him. That's it, I've got to ask him, *sample* him,' Duncan said weakly, 'if I can get up the nerve.'

'It's your worry,' the other said, 'but you better take my – '

'There!' exclaimed Duncan, pointing across the restaurant. 'He's getting up to go, and look at them all! They're all up, and he's in the middle, of course.'

'I don't see anybody.'

'I'm going to follow him some more. And when I get a chance – ' Duncan ran for the change counter.

Long shadows were falling on the waterfront. Hal would end his Walk here, where the city had its beginnings in the old whaling days. He passed between two warehouses and felt the boards of a pier springing under his feet. Small boats, dinghies, and a number of fishing-trawlers were slopping in the water. He woke slowly and mistily, as he had gone under, concentrating on bright things and sharp little sounds – the debris of life. Seagulls darted through the air. The water was rainbowed with oil and filled with orange peel, chips, crates, innertubes, bottles, and hunks of cork. There was a rhythmic groaning of stretched and relaxed rope. The wind blew, and whips of spray flew over the pier.

'Hi, hi!' A voice hailed him, and he saw the boy bent over like a question mark galloping out of the mists, with the pages of his clip board all tattered and flying like pennants. The pitiful and fanatic face confronted him; the scientific face, in which naïveté and knowledge struggled to prove something, peered at him.

'Pardon me!'

'Shoot,' he said.

'I've got to ask you the questions.'

'Sure,' Hal said. 'No, I don't mind. Got a job. Go to church. Oh, I'd say point five times a week. Coffee. What? Four, five cups a day. Yes, I do. No, I don't. One pack. King-sized. Light. Long-playing. Rural to urban. The mayor? Moderately. Read fewer books. Like to stay home. TV, I guess. Everybody has a right to their opinion, if they don't abuse it. Guilty. Yes, yes. Capital punishment. How many times? How many times? With us, it's two point three a week.'

Hal moved off. A shout followed him.

'My God!'

With desperate flourishes, the young scientist was totting up the score. 'I knew it. You gave me all the mean answers! Right down the line. Please, tell me who you work for!' he called in vain after the one in the slanted hat. 'What's your system? What are you doing in this town anyway?'

Hal didn't look back. Leaving the pollster in his windy solitude, he headed for the hotel to rest up for his invasion of the city in the morning.

14

The Rape of Bradford

Hal moved along with the crowds on Scupper Street. It was a mild morning, dry and bright. A formation of little woolly clouds had spread over the city. They were like lambs in the sky. All the people too reminded him of lambs, jostling and baa-ing in their concrete pasture. Strange that he had always thought of people as wild animals. Now he smiled at their helplessness. He already had two signed contracts in his pocket.

George Mack, the coal-dealer, had suddenly felt the need for a twenty-thousand-dollar annuity. Mack was talkative. He had insisted on telling Hal all about a crazy friend of his in Riverton, and made him promise to visit this man. But then he became aware of the wide-mouthed personality, the replica of himself being offered across the desk, and went limp with satisfaction. Similarly, the druggist with the long name wanted to apologize for being unable to take out more than ten thousand straight life. 'When business gets better, I'll call you, Hal,' he promised. Actual selling-time for both these prospects had been less than twenty minutes.

In Boston he had wondered whether Centralism might pay off only in happiness, and not in money. The possibility had worried him so that he had hardly dared think about it. Now it was clear there there were no limits to his power. Old Modesto's magic formula also worked in terms of cash. He stepped back into a doorway, apraising the passers-by. 'At the rate I'm going,' he thought, 'in one day I could make a fortune in commissions.'

The idea filled him with uneasy excitement. It was a deliberate violation of the WORK CENTRALLY commandment, but he could do it. He had the power to make enough money today so that he would never have to worry again. Lie around, go to Florida . . . He put it away from him. Ambition was the enemy. He went back into the crowd and resumed his walk. But now among all the round eyes his were like slits. One easy mark after another passed by. He felt his selling potential rise with each prospect. Some day he might lose this magic. Why not go after them now?

He looked at the people on the sidewalk. They had become his brothers and sisters. But they might change without warning. 'These gentle faces used to sneer at me,' he remembered. People were treacherous. If a man lost his strength, they turned on him and laughed at him, unless he had a reserve of honor in the bank.

Before he knew it he walked up to a carpenter in front of a cigar store, and backed him into a corner. Was his life built on a solid foundation? In seconds he piled a houseful of arguments around this one so that he couldn't escape. His hands shaped the cases and stories of the sale. He hammered his points home, sawed with his arms, and framed the little truths in their proper places, until the bewildered man stood looking at the four walls of his life, saying: 'Gee, I never thought of it that way,' and slowly drew out his fountain pen.

He looked around for another prospect, and another. He wanted to insure them all against everything, seize his chance – in a few hours make up a lifetime of failure! First he decided to go back to the hotel and fill his suitcase with policies. He hurried there. His pale, amiable face attracted no attention. They didn't know him, or what he could do.

At first he made appointments, after a fashion. He went to offices at random and asked to see the boss. No receptionist turned him away. Nor did the surprised and irritated men who reluctantly granted him what they supposed would be a minute or two. He sold them whatever policies he liked, regardless of their needs, and got up smiling and left while the ink was drying on their signatures. They followed him out of their offices, asking to see him again. The receptionists gazed after him as he disappeared into the elevators.

But it was too slow. Each success was taking him four or five minutes. He began to call on ground-floor storekeepers. He sold his policies with such speed that their faces became a blur. He went down the block, in and out of one store after another, changing his personality so quickly that for stretches at a time he forgot who he was and what he was trying to prove. It didn't matter. He was free at last. He had the wild and curious sensation of being in flight, of having cut loose from humanity. He had become a process in the shape of a man, and this was the marvelously logical conclusion of his kind of life.

Soon, even more logically, he was buttonholing his prospects on the street. His tempo increased. His personality changes came faster and faster until it seemed that he was putting on a street charade of all humanity. At the corner of Pike and Bond streets he started running from one person to another. He no longer bothered with persuasion. He was obtaining a signature every ninety seconds. By five o'clock it was a frenzy, a perfect orgy of selling in which, finally, he did not speak at all but had only to make a convulsive gesture and the peopele accepted the contracts he thrust at them.

This went on through the five-o'clock rush hour into the early hours of darkness, until all his policy forms were exhausted. Then, carrying his loaded suitcase, he staggered off to the park. He sat down on a bench and put his head in his hands.

He woke up. Somebody was poking him, and a voice said: 'Looks like he slept here all night.' The soft weight in his ribs was a broom. He saw the little white cart, the street-cleaner, and then the policeman. The two men were gazing down at him sympathetically.

'Move over, laddy, all I want is that paper under you there,' the street-cleaner said.

He was lying on an old newspaper in the park. He jumped to his feet. It was still rather dark, and the early-morning haze was like a veil before his eyes. The policeman's soft red Irish face seemed kind, as did the peaked countenance of the whitewing.

'Thank you, my boy,' said the street-cleaner, flourishing a sort of pike, and he speared the paper and dropped it in his portable trash can.

'What am I doing here?' Hal asked. In the distance, beyond the gurgling fountain, he saw the Leviathan Hotel, where he should have spent the night.

'Don't ask *us*,' said the policeman, 'suppose you tell us,' and the street-cleaner nodded. As it grew lighter, furtive shapes darted from the park in all directions.

'I don't know . . . I had a suitcase.'

'Behind you, lad.'

'Yes, here.' He knelt down and showed them. 'Life-insurance policies. I'm a salesman.'

'And a very good one too,' remarked the policeman, flashing his light on the papers, and pushing them with his nightstick. 'Every blasted one is filled out.'

A bell crashed six times, and the park was quiet again except for the rushing of water in the fountain. He remained on his knees by the suitcase, staring at its contents. The two public servants stood against the wet black grass and streaked sky, and watched him. They wanted to help him, but there was no help. The dawn made a negative of his life and showed him what he had done. The signed policies seemed to him a heap of ashes in the suitcase. He thought: 'For that, I've exchanged my life.' He didn't even feel sorry or afraid. Everything was hopeless, and he felt remote from his crime.

'I broke the law,' he said.

'What's this, now?' laughed the policeman. 'The city wouldn't enforce the statute against a nice fellow like you.'

He thanked them. They were nice little men who had nothing to do with him. They were talking about him as if he weren't there.

'The boy's a little sick in the head!' the street-cleaner was whispering. 'You better take him in to the Psycho ward. But use tact on him, Jimmy. Don't hurt his feelings.'

'I can see that you are no ordinary bum, but my friend thinks you might be needing a doctor. Will you come along?'

He would be glad to. He walked beside the policeman and the whitewing, who carried the suitcase on his cart. 'I'll tell you what,' said the policeman. 'Give me a few dollars, and I'll send this bag of yours to your company by parcel post. In your condition at present, you might lose it all.'

'All right,' he said. A transparent wall separated him from the world. He could reach and speak through it, but not get through it, nor care about anyone on the other side. Did they care for him?

'Sure they do.' The doctor smiled. 'Look. Physically, you're in fine shape. You've had a bit of a breakdown from overwork, that's all. It's nothing to be afraid of. The veil or wall you keep mentioning is absolutely in your imagination. Just don't think about it. The mind controls the body – you know that, don't you?'

'Yes, sir.' He sensed a game, and that this man was off somewhere playing it with himself.

'Now what is this so-called crime that worries you?'

'I broke the law.'

'Nonsense. Forget that, now. You're the kind of guy who needs to be with people. Be more with people. Don't stay alone and brood. When you get this feeling again, go out and talk to somebody. Your problem is to stay happy.'

'But I am – '

'Fine. You'll be all right.'

He wrote to Dr Modesto, without a heading: 'I HAVE VIOLATED WORK CENTRALLY,' and put down his return address as the Circle Hotel in Boston. He then dashed off another message. It was a love-letter to his fiancée. *Dear Rose.* Rose? One's fiancée was a thin little girl standing beside an X-ray machine, waiting for him. *I have not written before because I have been so busy making a go.* At any rate, he wasn't suffering any pain. He would try to go along, as if nothing had happened in Bradford. *Of things here.* But why didn't he care about anyone? *How are you, dear?* He got along with people effortlessly, but they didn't count. *I have missed you.* His pen scratched across the hotel stationery as he wrote the words of love. *I think of you a lot, and wish you could be here. However, it will not be so long, so don't worry. I have made a success in Bradford, and am going on to Riverton, as planned. Sometimes I dream of the cottage, and imagine you behind the picket fence. I mean, it could happen.*

He inserted *much* in front of *love.*

15

Rewards of Faith

'Isn't there a song called "Rose in Bloom?"' said Mr Brewster. 'I'm positive I've heard it.'

'What?' said Rose, eyeing the instrument panel. 'Now, will you please not move.'

'You are a very unresponsive young lady,' sighed the patient, turning his melancholy eyes on her. He lay naked on the X-ray table except for a loin cloth which appeared to fit his round body like a diaper.

'I don't mean to be, Mr Brewster, but – '

'And must it still be "Mr Brewster"? You couldn't call me "Jack"?'

'No, I don't think so. After all, you're a patient, and you're a college teacher. I'm not your type anyway.'

'Good lord, Rose! Can you honestly believe after we've chatted here so many times that I'm in some way different – particularly from one who is a specialist in her own right?'

'Even if you weren't different, you're married,' she told him, feeling ashamed and angry. 'Please don't talk. I'm going to take the picture.'

'Happily married! What a child you are!' the patient whispered.

She had hurt him. 'I'm sorry, Mr Brewster.' He smiled weakly as her fingertips brushed his shoulder. She lowered the crane over his abdomen. Once more at the panel, she called out: 'Don't breathe!' There was a long hum and a click. 'Good! That was just right. You can get dressed now.'

He lay still for a moment before getting up. He walked slowly to the chair where his clothes were folded. His deliberation annoyed Rose. Why couldn't he rush for his trousers like the others? Worse, he reached for his pipe instead of his trousers. Now he stood naked except for his peculiar underwear and the pipe in his mouth, looking at her quizzically.

'How old would you say I was?' he asked.

'Oh,' said Rose, turning away. 'Fifty, I should think.'

'Well, yes, as a matter of fact I *am* fifty,' Mr Brewster admitted with a sudden, loud laugh. 'But come on, now, that's not so old, is it?'

'I guess not,' Rose answered, still not wanting to look at him, but she smiled as she went into the darkroom and called back: 'Don't they say you're as old as you feel?'

'Exactly!' cried the almost naked pipe-smoker. 'And I feel thirty-five. You know, I sincerely fail to understand why I am not thirty-five, for all practical purposes.'

In the darkroom Rose lit a cigarette. She lifted Mr Brewster's first plate out of the solution and replaced it with the picture of his large intestine. She studied the shadow of the right kidney. It was a good film. Dr Warren would be pleased. She moved into the deepest black shadow and made her cigarette glow. The smoke drifted across the bar of dull blue fluorescent light that faintly illuminated the sink.

On the other side of the partition, Mr Brewster said: 'I seem to remember that you have a boy friend.'

'Yes,' she answered miserably. 'He's been away.' She had a boy friend who had not thought enough of her to send a postcard.

'Well, that's fine. You should. But I wonder if he would object to your having another – acquaintance, for cocktails and dinner occasionally, say, at the Copley Plaza, and then an evening at Symphony Hall, or if you prefer lighter things – ' Mr Brewster's laughter penetrated her dark closet – 'some kind of vaudeville show.'

She crushed out her cigarette. His soft voice depressed her, yet undoubtedly he would be kind. She recalled a saying that mature men appreciated you more.

He was waiting for her with his hat in his hand, a plump, not-so-old figure in seersucker. 'Well, good-bye until next time.' He smiled.

'Mr Brewster!' Rose seized his hand. 'I wish I could. The thing is, even if he hasn't written, he will any day, and I wouldn't feel right – I guess I'm the old-fashioned type.'

He touched her cheek. 'Rose, your kind is always in fashion, thank God. Now, you say you've received no word from him lately? Never mind. His letter will come. Young men can be thoughtless.

You have to expect that. As the years go by, they gradually learn tenderness. Meanwhile, until things are all right again, may I not offer you – ' Mr Brewster bowed good-humoredly – 'the dubious pleasure of having dinner with me tonight?'

'No,' thought Rose. 'I can't. It's the first step down.' She found herself reacting to the pressure of his fingers.

'Don't answer now if you don't want to,' he said. 'I have it. You go home and think about the idea. I'll phone you at seven. Let's make up a code. When you answer my call, if you'd like an evening of talk and music, say: 'Yes, Jack.' If not, well, I suppose – ' he made a charming gesture – 'it will have to be "Mr Brewster." *Au revoir*, Rose.'

'*Au* – good-by,' she stammered, as the door closed softly between them.

She went home and found Hal's letter in the mailbox, and read it several times before going upstairs. It didn't matter that the message was short. At least he was not afraid to put his love in writing. She climbed the stairs with a feeling of relief.

There was, she thought, something sad about the letter. The lifeless handwriting in pale blue ink seemed that of a stranger patiently fulfilling his obligations. This didn't trouble her. She had been doing a lot of thinking since he had gone, and realized that his air of lifelessness was what appealed to her. He was not an animal like the others. Even on their one romantic night, he had not forced his desire on her in an obsessed or ugly way. Rather he had slipped in with a muttered apology, as if to say: 'Is this place taken?' and consummated their engagement courteously, without fuss.

In the bedroom Gladys's clothes had been flung into every corner. She had evidently finished packing for her trip to Maine, where she was to join Heffernan for a week. The football-player was working in a sawmill operated by Bay State coach Ed Notsik, to toughen himself for the fall campaign.

Gladys had been entertaining. The sink was filled with coffee cups and glasses containing wet cigarette butts. Rose sighed and began to clean up. While rinsing the dishes, she considered again the strange race of males that women had to deal with. They were all operators – all, sooner or later, after one thing. Some, like Johnny Heffernan, came after you stamping and knocking things over. Soft little brutes, Mr Brewster's kind, sneaked in with sympathy. Whatever kind they were, they remained the privileged characters to be placated, cajoled, somehow held off.

The downstairs door slammed in a way that announced Gladys's arrival. There was a good deal of scraping on the staircase, and the front door flew open, admitting Gladys. Behind her came a wobbling tower of football equipment carried by a small, disappointed man with a sharp face.

'Put it here, Swan,' said Gladys. 'No, wait. In the other room!'

It was too late. The tower swayed and fell over. Cleats, shoulder pads, a helmet and nose guard tumbled to the floor.

'You might have waited.'

'How could I help it? You change your mind at the last moment.'

Gladys took a load into the bedroom, explaining to Rose: 'Johnny needs it. They're going to practice up there.'

'Who's *that*?' asked Rose, with a giggle.

'Oh, Swan – my roommate, Rose. Rose – Swan.'

'I'm pleased to meet you,' said Swan. 'Look, Gladys. I should be going now. Whether you appreciate it or not, I've got work to do.'

'Well, we aren't chaining you, my dear boy.'

Swan scowled and lit a cigarette. 'I assumed that you might want to say good-by to me,' he said.

'All right, then, good-bye!' called Gladys from the other room. 'Thanks for your ass-istance.'

Swan stood up furiously and marched from the room. At the door he hesitated, and said loudly: 'You might have the kindness to let me know when you get back!'

The phone rang, and Rose answered it.

'Remember our code,' said a melodious voice.

'What?'

'Our code, my dear. Who am I?'

'Oh,' said Rose. 'Mr Brewster.'

There was a silence, and then the voice at the other end said: 'Well, really. Are you sure it isn't *Jack*?'

'No, no, Mr Brewster.' She wanted to laugh, and yet she pitied him.

'It does seem to me – I've already bought tickets – I'm entitled . . .' She laid the receiver gently on the table. The voice buzzed on until finally the hornet died.

When Gladys asked who it was, she laughed. 'That pest!'

* * *

The trustees and alumni of the Browning & Snow School of Business Administration applauded. Fred Purdy inclined his head toward various parts of the hall. His cheeks were darkly flushed. Like everyone else in the room, he was sweating. His linen coat had wilted. His pants were soggy and splashed with beer. What did that matter? More beer! He reached for his stein and took a long swig. Most of his listeners did the same, and a clatter of crockery hit the tables.

'Name your own moral!' Fred Purdy said. 'All I know is, my rabbit turned into a tiger. Mind you, we aren't claiming any miracles yet. The boy is undisciplined. We'll have to throw out most of those Bradford contracts. Even so, he's set a record – and remember, he's just starting.'

He looked around the hall and saw that they were well pleased with him. Now for the cliché that would put them at rest.

'Why did his conversion take place? In my opinion, Hingham found *belief* in his job . . .'

He elaborated on this untruth for several minutes more, and sat down, bowing to their thunderous appreciation. But he would not bow to the romance he had just invented. He had not, of course, filled Hingham with faith. In a fit of irritation, he had tried to knock the last bit of 'belief' out of him. What troubled Purdy was that he might actually have inspired Hingham without meaning to.

He shrugged off their glad hands and went out on the fire escape for a smoke. 'Unbelief is the first step toward freedom,' he said to himself. He had always meant this as an angry joke.

'Purdy! Purdy!' they were calling. 'Where's Fred Purdy?'

He tossed away his smoke and returned to the world of beer and good fellowship.

The Revelations
of Dr Modesto

PART TWO

16

The Athletic Crowd

It was a cool blue Fourth of July morning in Riverton. People were hurrying through the streets in sports costumes, carrying picnic lunches, tennis rackets, beach umbrellas, and guitars. On every street one heard firecrackers. A fife-and-drum corps was marching somewhere. Through this atmosphere of aggressive gaiety and good health ran the dogged young athlete Hal Hingham. He was dressed in flannels and a white sports shirt, and he wore white sneakers. In one hand he carried a tennis racket, in the other a canvas bag. The bag contained a white sweater, some tennis balls, gauze tape, and iodine.

He ran as fast as he could, occasionally looking back over his shoulder, as if he hoped to run out from under his sin. In this healthy town he would be an athlete. If he hid among the clean young people of Riverton, perhaps what he had done in Bradford would not catch up with him. This was his plan. Yet he didn't really care whether it worked – if only he could get back to life. He felt as if he were closed away from everybody. The air around him was like glass, and he felt like knocking on it, to let himself out, so that he could be with other people. He was a sunburned tennis-player without a partner.

He hoped to find one, for he was on his way to the Riverton Olympic Club to disappear among the athletes. He was looking for George Mack's old friend Tim Ashburn. The Bradford coal-dealer had made a point of it. 'You'll get a kick out of him,' he said. 'Tim's a funny guy. He'll do anything for you if you make him feel young. He's got a youth compelex.'

Before selling the coal-dealer his annuity, Hal had listened to the story of Tim Ashburn.

Tim Ashburn decided on his forty-fifth birthday that he was not going to get any older. He meant this in absolute seriousness. By regular feats of prowess, like the boy who lifted the calf every day, he, Tim Ashburn, would prove to others and to his own body that he was *de facto* no older than he had been the week before. Systematically he went about remaining young. First, he surrounded himself with young people. Secondly, he made it his mission to beat young men, and young women, at their own games. 'He's had four wives.' Mack grinned. 'Wore 'em all out. Every girl he marries is younger than the last one.'

Tim learned all the crazy new dances. He got himself on supervisory committees of the high-school proms – then showed up at the dances and out-jitterbugged everybody. He refused to let his wives have children, for fear of aging unconsciously as the kids grew up around him. And always he competed with young men. As president of the Whitestone Mill, where most of them worked, he had them at his genial mercy. He was able to force them into competition, beat them year after year, and so prove once more and again that Tim Ashburn had made time stand still.

He made his eternal youth a matter of record. He did this by founding the Riverton Olympic Club. Twice a year the Club held an 'Olympic Games.' And every year, winter and summer, Tim Ashburn somehow whipped the younger generation.

'The Fourth of July is when they have their summer games,' Mack said. 'If you want to do business with Tim, get in on one of the events and lose to him.'

After Bradford, business was the last thing he wanted to do. It would be months before he could try to sell any more insurance. Perhaps never, he thought.

Hal trotted on to the grounds of the Riverton Olympic Club. Young men and girl athletes were rambling across the turf, high-jumping, throwing the discus, putting the shot, and racing down the cinder track. Tanned boys of violent beauty lifted bar bells. Others climbed into pyramids. Across the field bronzed figures could be seen plying canoes on a small lake.

Hal went into the clubhouse. He arrived in time to hear a worried-looking boy shout over the loudspeaker system:

'Winner of the raft-paddle is – MR ASHBURN!'

This announcement resounded from amplifiers all over the field. A man walked past Hal and flung himself panting into a deck chair. He gazed with a taut smile at the scoreboard, watching the boy chalk up a '10' in the space where the 'Raft-Paddle' and 'Ashburn' columns intersected. He mopped his crew-cut gray hair. There were no lines on his face, but the skin was drawn tight over his cheekbones. He appeared masked and ageless, with only the bright and rather unpleasant eyes alive, ironically, with the desperation of age. He nodded to Hal, who introduced himself.

'A friend of George's, eh? I see you're dressed up to exercise,' Tim Ashburn said.

Hal felt under pressure, and he understood what this man wanted. Tim Ashburn had to put him down, because he was young and held a tennis racket in his hand. It was nothing personal, but a matter of his host's survival. As Ashburn looked him over, with the challenging and unpleasant smile, he felt that he was being competitively searched and probed for weak points. What a pleasure it would be to lose to such a man! Hal imagined how much Ashburn would like him after beating him. ('Well, boy, you were good, but not quite good enough.' – 'Yes, sir. I did my best.' – 'No disgrace in that.') Again he experienced the fine, warm Centralistic feeling – the comfort of being a second-rater. He could hardly wait to fling himself in happy defeat before his obsessed opponent.

'So tennis is your game. Are you any good?' Tim Ashburn asked.

'Well, I can give you a good game, I think.'

'Winner of the discus-throw – BIG DICK TRENT!' cried the scoreboard boy in a frightened tone, as Tim Ashburn glanced darkly at the results.

'Of course, the entries are closed,' he said to Hal. 'And you can't be a member, unless I make you one. Besides, only one man has dared to challenge me in tennis. Do you really think you'd have a chance, Hingham?'

'I believe I could give you a close battle, Mr Ashburn.'

The scoreboard boy turned his back, and announced that Big Dick Trent had won the shotput *and* the hammer-throw.

Tim Ashburn got slowly to his feet. 'Maybe we can get you in,' he said. 'Come on, boy. I'll show you around. I've still got time before my next event.' As they went out the door, he laughed and pushed Hal roughly on the shoulder.

They strolled among the athletes, and Hal noticed that every- where they went a way was parted for them, and they were alone. The young people bowed with uneasy friendliness to the savagely smiling man who kept young by beating them, and retreated from him. They seemed cowed by his presence. But behind his back some of the young men regarded Tim Ashburn sullenly, and the girls laughed at him. The founder of the Riverton Olympic Club knew nothing of this. He continued to walk proudly in the bright light of noon with his head held high, so that no one could say that his neck was wrinkled.

'Winner of the girls' hundred-yard dash – JOAN VIGORO. Time: twelve seconds flat!'

'That's good time,' said Hal.

'Too good. Look at her.' Tim Ashburn nodded toward a tall, limber girl with a darkly attractive, unhappy face. She was being clapped on the back by enthusiastic muscular boys, who immediately turned away from her and gave their attention to the girls who had lost the race. Hal felt sorry for her, although, of course, he agreed with the fellows that a girl athlete shouldn't expect any attention. Joan Vigoro picked up her sweater. She went off by herself and sat disconsolately on a pile of boards.

'She's too good for a girl. I mean twelve seconds flat,' said Tim Ashburn. '*I* only run the hundred in eleven flat. Now take my wife – her best time is twelve eight.'

Hal nodded. 'That's more like it.'

'Everybody out for the rope-skipping!'

'Well, parm me now, I'm going to win my specialty,' said Tim Ashburn. 'Why don't you run over and talk to Joan? She needs a good man. So long, pal, I mean Hal.' He winked, and the raillery of his enforced youth seemed even more horribly unnatural as he hustled off to join the boys.

'Miss Vigoro,' said Hal, 'congratulations,' and he didn't know what to say when she blushed and smiled at him. The show of gratitude made her prettier. Hal thought how popular she might become if only she would not run so fast. But in a moment she was the lonely and unwanted girl again. Lack of confidence made her awkward. As she stood before him, hot and disheveled from her victory, she couldn't think of anything feminine to do, and coughed with adolescent gruffness, and looked away, twirling her sweater.

'Why are you so sad? Why do you stay by yourself?' he asked.

Joan looked at him. 'Because I do my best!' she exclaimed bitterly. 'That's why they leave me alone. I don't care. I'll run as fast as I can, whatever they think. It's the only way I can be myself.'

She was, of course, making a terrible mistake.

'Oh yes,' Joan went on. 'The fellows like to play games with me, but they go home with the other girls. Why? Is there some law of nature that I can't be myself with a man?'

Hal tried to explain. 'You could take it a little easy . . .'

'Am I attractive?'

'Yes, but a lot of fellows, you know, they like to relax with a girl, and not – '

'You're just like the others!' cried Joan Vigoro. 'There must be a man somewhere who . . . When I run, I run! When I jump, I jump as high as I can. All the fellows beat me anyway. Why don't they let me practice with them, and then take me out? I want a man – like Big Dick. I hope he beats the old man today – but why does a guy like that hang around Doris Michaels? Look at her over there, with those fellows. She came in *last*. And now I'm all alone in the girls' high jump – '

'Girls' high jump,' a bored voice announced. 'Canceled!'

Joan explained: 'That's the new rule. If nobody will compete against you, you don't get the points – not even by default. The old man fixed it so – '

'Winner of the rope-skipping – MR ASHBURN!'

'I don't care any more!' said Joan, and Hal realized that she was crying. 'I'm going to shame them all. Do you know how? I'll shame myself – I've already fixed it!'

A small brown knot-headed youth approached Hal. 'I'm Fred Watt,' he said. 'The old – Mr Ashburn wants to see you.'

'Please,' Hal said to Joan. 'Take it easy now. I'll see you later.'

'I'll tell you at the party,' she promised. 'I'll tell them all.'

'I'm not very strong yet. Not like Big Dick,' said Fred Watt. 'But I can bend a coke cap between my thumb and forefinger. Can you?' He produced one.

Hal said he had to save his strength for tennis. Watt glanced at him curiously: 'That's funny. I thought Hank Watson – ' He stopped and breathed: 'Look at him!' He was gazing rapturously at a lazy blond giant poised for a javelin throw.

'Big Dick Trent?' Hal inquired.

'Yeah.'

Pythons seemed to coil and uncoil beneath Big Dick's polished skin. He threw the javelin and it disappeared, amid a murmur from the girl athletes.

Hal heard a familiar voice, and saw Tim Ashburn horseshoe-pitching. He was talking what at first seemed to be nonsense to a comely girl spectator, making complicated wind-ups and tossing a shoe, shouting back over his shoulder, pitching another. 'See that, honey!' he shouted. 'That's the one. Oop! Just missed, almost a leaner. Look! Look at me, now! I'm going to ring the next one for sure!'

Hal learned that the girl was Tim's new wife, and the reason for the uproar he was creating became clear. Tim was watching her watch Big Dick Trent, and consequently missing his shots.

'Hey, honey! We're sixteen all. Look, now. Are you with me? Got to make it. Got to make a ringer!' His shouts were in vain. Big Dick Trent had come sauntering by, and all the girls, including his own wife, were turning to the young god like so many flowers.

With a groan, Tim Ashburn let fly his horseshoe. The crucial toss was wide and short, but it landed on the rim, and then miraculously leaped and rolled erratically to the stake and fell over for a ringer, while the amazed victor danced and tore at his aged crew-cut in a frenzy of joy, repeating: 'Yes! Yes!' and two officials, one from the horsehoe pit and the other from the cluster of javelin-throwers, dashed for the clubhouse.

'Winner of the javelin-throw – DICK TRENT!'

'Winner of the horseshoe-pitching is – MR ASHBURN!'

There was a pause. A noise of embarrassment came over the public address system: 'The points are – leaders, Trent, forty-six, er, Ashburn, forty-four, but there will be a – delay,' the voice concluded, and a painful silence ensued.

Still breathing in gasps, but triumphant, Tim Ashburn assured his wife: 'Don't think anything of it, honey. Remember I have the tennis, with Hank Watson. What are you laughing at?'

'Isn't that the little one I beat 6–1 last month?'

'Perhaps so, but he's a man and has a right to challenge me.'

All eyes turned toward a runner arriving from the clubhouse. It was Fred Watt.

'Hank Watson quit!' he yelled. 'He won't play tennis! No point for tennis! The new champion is Big Dick Trent!'

If he expected pandemonium, he was disappointed. The members of the Riverton Olympic Club backed away in silence, leaving the premature revolutionist alone to face Tim Ashburn. Fred Watt's eyes rolled wildly, but the founder of the Olympic Club paid no attention to him.

'Stay here with Eleanor!' Tim Ashburn whispered to Hal, indicating his wife, and strode away in the direction of the clubhouse, followed at a distance by the mob of athletes he had held in subjection for so long.

Hal and Eleanor Ashburn looked at each other.

'Somebody pulled a double-cross,' she said meditatively, 'and somebody's losing his grip.'

Hal felt a plucking at his elbow, and a voice asked: 'You wanna wrestle?'

He turned to find a small ox of a man eying him forlornly. This one's muscles looked like so many motionless boulders. He seemed in danger of splitting his skin whenever he moved.

'No, he can't wrestle. He's our boy. He's going to play tennis,' said Eleanor Ashburn, taking Hal's arm.

'Gee, Mrs Ashburn . . .'

'Lumpy, you're just too strong for your own good,' she laughed.

The would-be wrestler blinked under his low hairline. 'Aw, there's no competition for a guy,' he said finally. 'I ain't going to hang around here. I'm going home probably.'

He walked away. Eleanor Ashburn and Hal started toward the clubhouse, where the crowd of athletes waited. She explained that he had been challenged by Lumpy Modoc, the strongest man, possibly excepting Big Dick, in the city. As a youth he had been sensitive about his five feet five inches, and built himself into an impossible physical specimen. He had taken every lesson in jiujitsu, trained for years with a Japanese until he could even beat his instructor. In all these years Lumpy had never had a chance to use jiujitsu on anyone, because all men were polite to him. He was desperate to wrestle, but fated never to have a chance.

'Why doesn't Big Dick wrestle with him?' Hal asked.

'And spoil that beautiful body! No one could expect him to do anything like that, not even Lumpy,' Eleanor answered scornfully.

There was a commotion at the clubhouse, and the announcement blared from the amplifier on the roof:

'Final event of the day! Tennis, two sets out of three! Guest member Hal Hingham of Boston versus – MR ASHBURN!'

* * *

As Hal and Tim Ashburn rallied for service, the stands were packed with members of the Olympic Club. They were silent, and Hal felt the weight of their despair. He drove to Tim Ashburn's forehand and backhand, and found them steady. Lobs did not bother him, nor volleys touch his smiling equanimity. He tested him with a drop shot, and this worked. His opponent flubbed it into the net. He chopped, and Tim Ashburn lunged ineffectually at another short, back-spinning ball.

This was the secret of Tim Ashburn's weakness! Now he would most carefully lose to the aging dictator by feeding him gentle, deep drives to his strength.

But even as he did so, and Tim Ashburn passed him with shot after shot, Hal's conscience began to bother him. He sensed an enormous hostility in the stands directed toward 'the old man.' Shouldn't he then change his point of view, thrash Ashburn, and free the Olympic Club from the domination of the man who refused to grow old? Somehow he knew this was wrong. For along with their hatred of Tim Ashburn, the members still expected him to win and lead them. They griped at his legend, yet needed it. They would be shocked if he were toppled – even though they resented him. Because he and his brand of physical culture had corrupted them. If Tim Ashburn were to lose, life would undergo a drastic and frightening change. The Olympic Club might be abolished, and the freed slaves *wouldn't know what to do with their bodies*.

Thus Hal rationalized it, and went on to a decent defeat. He knew the joys of the John The Baptist Complex, the eternal Number Two Man's cry: 'I am good, but, oh, I am not fit to tie the winner's shoelaces!' It was close, honorable, fine. They went 7–5 and 5–7. Now it was 6–5 in Tim Ashburn's favor, Tim's service, 40–30, match point. Pow! The man who refused to grow old had aced him in the blazing sunlight. He shook his head ruefully. 'Never saw it!' The victor was hurdling the net.

Hal shook hands with Tim Ashburn and wandered over to the sideline for a drink of water. As he splashed cold water on his face, a girl went by without looking at him.

'Hey, I'm here,' he laughed weakly.

'Are you?' she said. 'You could have beaten him.'

It was Joan Vigoro, and she was right. As a person, he was now only an optical illusion.

Regretting her rudeness, she came back and laid her hand on his arm. 'Never mind. What you did was better for *them*,' she said, with a contemptuous gesture toward the Olympic Club members. She added in a fierce undertone: 'See me at the party, and I'll tell you – '

Voices from across the court summoned him.

'Hey, boy!'

'Come on, Hal!'

He went along to watch the ceremonies. Sullenly they crowned Tim Ashburn with a laurel wreath. He stood with his sweaty ageless arms around pretty Eleanor. She no longer had eyes for Big Dick Trent, because the old man had done it again for one more year.

The victory party was a mild affair. Once this group of athletes came indoors, they appeared to be shackled by their muscles. As conversation lapsed, the club members' attention strayed to their muscles and those of others. They stroked their own arms and legs. Big Dick Trent carefully examined every inch of himself for minute abrasions that might mar his golden skin.

As usual, Joan Vigoro sat alone. She caught Hal's eye and beckoned to him. She waited moodily, with her arm around the silver cup she had won as champion of the girls' division.

'I've made up my mind!' she whispered. 'Listen!'

'No, you mustn't,' Hal said, after she told him. Even though she wasn't his type, and he didn't care to be seen talking with her for too long, he thought her plan was a shame. But she insisted.

Men wouldn't let her be herself. They ignored and rejected her, and made her feel ugly. It was unnatural to run fast. All right, then. She was going to the other extreme. She would give up *all* her pride. She had written to a Lonely Hearts Club, offering herself as a bride to anyone who would have her. She would never high-jump again, or run again, but would devote herself exclusively to cooking and household drudgery.

'I have an answer,' she told him. 'A horrible old man, and I'm going to marry him.'

Hal couldn't stand her suffering. 'All right,' he said angrily, 'if you won't take my advice, go ahead and be a fool,' and turned his back on Joan Vigoro.

Gray-faced Tim Ashburn left, leaning on his wife's arm. The party started to find its natural outlet in physical feats. A man with ropy ankles inserted his feet under a wall radiator. He leaned backwards with his body straight and stiff, hanging on only by his ankles, and went down, slowly as a minute hand, until he was flat on the floor. Then he lifted himself just as slowly to an upright position.

The applause was interrupted by a crew-cut boy who appeared at the door and shouted: 'Lumpy Modoc has found somebody who wants to fight! A guy outside has *challenged* him!'

Everybody rushed into the street.

17

The Death of Jiujitsu

'What happened?' Hal asked Fred Watt, who had seen it all.

'They bumped on the sidewalk. This guy . . .'

Lumpy had quit the athletic grounds in disgust because another Olympic had gone by and nobody had given him a chance to use his jiujitsu. 'What's the use of learning it if everybody's scared?' he complained. Just the same, he was still only five feet five inches tall. He stayed that way, and they could still look down on him. Girls to. He could lift them with one hand, but they were taller. 'Nobody to practice holds with since the Jap quit,' he grumbled. It was so bad sometimes he actually wrestled with himself, although there was little satisfaction in that. As he trudged away from the clubhouse waving his arms and complaining, the astonishing thing happened.

'This guy . . .' said Fred Watt, pointing to him excitedly. 'He just elbowed Lumpy in the ribs, and he says: "Watch out where you're going, you ape!"'

Hal saw Lumpy shoulder to shoulder with a small, angry man. This fellow stood about five feet six. He didn't look very strong. His face was weathered and knobbed like a fist. Bright black eyes considered Lumpy with unendurable contempt. He was dressed in blue jeans, white sash, and red shirt, but this was his only concession to the holiday spirit. He was mean, and asking for it. He spat in the gutter and said: 'Why don't you get back in your cage?'

The athletic crowd surrounded them, talking it up, and Hal was the first to call out: 'Go get him, Lump!'

'Put up your fists!' said Lumpy Modoc, trembling with joy.

The little man came at him.

Lumpy picked him up and threw him over his shoulder. He seized him by the leg and sent him cartwheeling against a brick wall. The little man dropped, and Lumpy methodically shattered his head on the pavement, propped him against the wall, cuffed his neck, and batted his Adam's apple. He released him. Absurdly, his adversary remained upright. Then Lumpy blinked from a right to the jaw, and stopped for a few seconds to consider this punch.

'Go get him!'

Lumpy corkscrewed the little man's wrist and waved him like a flag. He threw him he knew not where or how far, and there was the screech of automobile brakes. The athletes swung around in amazement to see the little man crawl from underneath the car and come shambling back for more.

Lumpy glanced distrustfully at his biceps, and a small suspicion appeared to enter his mind. Forgetting his science, he rushed at the little man and knocked him down four times. In between the second and third knockdown he received a cruel kick in the shins. There were fists in his eyes. He took a tremendous, enraged breath, and – too late – realized that the indestructible head was diving at him. He couldn't harden his solar plexus in time. A canonball quaked in his stomach. He drifted along the sidewalk, his legs ambling in various directions. He approached the lamp post slowly, and gave up. He hit gently, and collapsed.

In silence the crowd made way for the little red, white, and blue turkeycock of a man, who strutted off toward the center of town.

Lumpy Modoc's sobbing filled the locker room. *The first time!* he moaned. Hal wound the gauze around his bloody head. He could give no sympathy to the humiliated strong boy, after noticing the contempt with which the other athletes turned their backs on him. He shrugged his shoulders and made a disparaging gesture to indicate that *somebody* had to care for the discredited one.

'Don't leave me!' begged Lumpy. He leaned his discolored head on Hal's shoulder. The bloody towels and bandages gave him the look of a broken swami. The others had gone, and now Hal soothed him: 'It could happen to anybody.' From far away he heard band music. 'Let's go watch the parade,' he suggested.

It was better out there with the fife-and-drum corps. Lumpy's spirits picked up. 'Gee, I'd like to play the drum,' he said. They followed a particularly magnificent bass drum to the Court House Square. Here they came upon thousands of people gazing skyward. They followed the community gaze, searching for parachutes or rockets, but saw nothing.

'Look at that crazy guy!'

'Where?' Hal demanded.

'There he is!' cried Lumpy, and Hal caught sight of a tiny figure *walking up the side of the courthouse*, without a rope to help him, without anything. His body was rigid, at right angles to the side of the building, yet he walked up and up, defying gravity itself. A human fly!

The incredible climber reached the golden spike on top of the courthouse dome, wrapped his legs around it, whirled, and waved his hat, as the applause went roaring up to him. Then he descended slowly, in measured steps, the same way, only this time facing down – and it could be observed that he was grinning – leaping finally into a shower of coins from the populace.

They pressed close, and then Hal heard Lumpy shout in terror: 'That's him! That's the guy!' and saw him run away. The crowd swept him toward a new experience, and he joined the people who were flinging dimes and quarters, and even fifty-cent pieces, into a large canvas trough. A placard fixed to this receptacle proclaimed: 'MERKO THE HUMAN FLY.'

18
The Human Fly

While the coins were still flying around him, Merko the Human Fly walked scowling to the canvas trough. He unwound a long leather cord, walked around to the other side of the receptacle, and with a mighty yank zippered the trough shut. Then, ignoring the spectators' gasps of admiration and the money thrown too late that pattered against the closed canvas, he heaved the great burden of coin onto his shoulders and marched out of the square.

The crowd followed him, and Hal followed the crowd. His heart was pumping and he was violently excited. He noticed how all the people did not press close to Merko. They milled in a wide circle around the little man, who refused to stagger under his huge sack. Merko strode on, his face contorting into a tighter and tighter knot of determination to *make it* wherever he was going, whatever for. Hal found that, like all the others, he had to run to keep up with Merko, who darted now into a side street, and then into a dead-end alley, and marched up to a seven-foot fence.

The crowd backed up. Embarrassment seized everybody, because the little man, for no reason except curiosity on their part, had been forced into this corner. But then he turned on them with a fierce look. Shouting a wordless oath, he swung the gigantic zippered trough as a hammer-thrower would, over the fence, and, still hanging on to it, disappeared, flung out of sight by his own feat.

Hal ran to the fence and tried vainly to climb it. He had to find Merko the Human Fly, catch him before he got away. He ran around the corner, searching every doorway, frightened at what kind of demon the miraculous climber must be to possess him so. A little man like nobody else he had ever seen. 'Yes, like nobody else,' he thought. 'I've got to talk to him.'

But there was no such person, Dr Modesto said. Merko had to be like somebody. Every man was a product of his town pattern, even a human fly. He tried to put himself in Merko's frame of mind in order to guess what direction he would have taken. It was no good. Just as he defied gravity, Merko seemed to escape Centralistic law.

He might have gone to the bank with all those coins. But it was a holiday. Then Hal noticed a fellow with an amazed expression, and rushed up to him.

'Did you see a little guy with a sackful of coins on his back?'

'*See* him? There he is, down that block, getting on the motorcycle.'

Timid and excited, he approached the motorcycle. It had a sidecar, into which Merko was stuffing the canvas trough. He glanced up at Hal, and went on with his task.

'Excuse me . . .'

The Human Fly didn't answer. He continued with furious, gloomy concentration to pound the sack deeper into the sidecar. Hal knew he would have to pour everything into centralizing this little man – to project his likeness in such a way that for Merko the very air would become a mirror. He watched him force the canvas into a space that nature had intended to be too small. Then Merko straddled the motorcycle. He kicked, and the engine roared and died.

Hal stepped up. Expressionlessly, indomitably, he handed the little man his card and said: 'I want to talk to you.'

The other scrutinized the card and put it in his pocket. He kicked the motor again, and over the roar shouted something at Hal.

'What?' Hal yelled. He couldn't read a yes or a no on the fist of a face vibrating before him. With a wild feeling, he climbed onto the load of canvas. He waited with his eyes shut for a push in the face, but was jolted instead by the roaring start of the motorcycle. He grasped what he thought was an iron bar, but which, moving, proved to be his companion's arm. They spun around a corner. Hal found the zipper cord on the canvas sack, and hung on. After a number of violent swerves the motorcycle reached the main road, and with one gunning acceleration they were out of town. Hal relaxed, as the steady roar became a sort of quiet. He glimpsed Merko's grim but not unkind face, his hair flung out behind him in the shape of a flat heart, his amazingly ungoggled eyes blasted by the wind but nevertheless gazing straight ahead, as teardrops whipped out of their corners, several of them wetting Hal's cheek.

Hal lay across the canvas mound of money. He felt almost sleepy. He imagined that they were in roaring flight towards a new world that would somehow be better for him. Only two or three minutes had gone by when he felt Merko's hand gripping his shoulder. The motorcycle swerved into a road full of rocks that jarred him to the eyeballs.

They came to a stop in a clearing on the slope of a small hill. The grass was dry and dusty, and the heat of the afternoon beat down on them. Hal waited for Merko to unload his money, but the little man only shook himself with a doglike motion and set off down a path circling the hill. Hal stayed with him. He offered Merko a cigarette.

'I'm not smoking.'

'You don't smoke.'

'I smoke when I want to. When I choose to want to,' said Merko in a harsh, flat voice.

'What can I say to him?' Hal wondered. 'They're bad for your wind, I guess,' he said.

'They would be,' returned his companion, 'if I let them.' Merko suddenly began to walk faster.

'Oh, I see . . .'

'No, you don't,' Merko declared in the same rigid tone that made Hal increasingly uneasy because he felt some terrible emotion behind it. 'I could smoke too much and *still* not let it get my wind.'

They walked on in silence. Now and then Merko spat on the grass. 'Unless I wanted to lose my wind,' he said, for the first time without being spoken to. They came to an upgrade. Ramming his hands in his pockets, Merko redoubled his pace. The steeper the grade, the faster he walked.

'How can you control – all that?' Hal panted.

'Will power!'

'But,' said Hal, as they plunged uphill, 'smoking is a physical thing.'

'So is will power,' said Merko through his clenched teeth.

Hal thought of Merko climbing up the side of the courthouse, and of his feats with the money trough. 'You know, you left your money back there,' he remembered.

Merko laughed. 'Who could lift it out?'

'Well, they might burn – '

'Asbestos.'

Hal had begun to feel emanations from this strange little man like nobody else. Glancing at his companion's knobbed face and hands, he exulted in the same maniacal concentration on not just walking but smashing a path through the air as he walked. *Will power was a physical thing.*

'I could do it,' he asserted emotionally, 'if I could just get the hang of it.'

'What?' Merko demanded harshly.

'Climb – '

'*That*,' Merko said. 'If you want to, you can.'

'Yes, once you get the hang of the law of gravity.'

'Gravity!' Merko laughed with contempt even for it. 'That doesn't make any difference. If you want to climb, just *go*,' he said with a ferocious and agonized grimace. He repeated in a fury: 'Go! That's all. Do it!'

'But what's the secret?'

'Punish yourself!' Merko declared passionately. 'Whip yourself. *Drive*. One slip and you're through.' He glared at Hal. 'Understand?'

'Yes, but – up the side of a building?'

'Drive, that's all.'

'Don't you use some kind of equipment?' Hal asked.

Merko sat down on the grass. He took off his sneakers and displayed small but incredibly muscled feet which he flexed like hands. He bent his left foot from the arch until the big toe touched the bottom of his heel.

'I'm no freak. I didn't have feet like these in the beginning. I used suction cups like all the others do. Or metal shoes and electromagnets – it's all the same fraud, because you're not doing it yourself. I knew that, and I wouldn't let myself be satisfied. I said: "I'll whip this."

'They laughed at me. They sounded just like you: "What are you going to do – repeal the law of gravity?" '

Hal drew away as the little man snarled up at him.

'As if that could stop me! I knew there had to be some way. Of course, I didn't know then that you can do *anything* you want.' Again Merko fixed his angry gaze on Hal, daring him to contradict this.

But Hal was with him. Will power was the answer. He felt himself under the spell of two powerful eyes. The little man thrust a spike-like finger at Hal's chest.

'When they laughed at me I went away. I went up on a mountain. A voice told me: "*Refuse* to be killed," and I threw myself off.'

'Off the mountain!'

'It was a precipice, with brush and brambles and rocks at the bottom. I hit on my pelvis. I broke my ribs and my jaw and one leg, *but I crawled home!*' Merko's shout echoed around the rocky hillside.

Out of habit Hal started to say: 'I'd do the same, we all would,' but the pathetic lie wouldn't come forth. 'You must have gone to the hospital,' he said feebly.

'That's right,' said Merko. 'I slept a week or two. Then I got up and went home, and I began my training. I started with my feet. I clasped irons on the toes and heels and flexed them two hours every day until they could do what I promised.'

'Your feet are their own suction cups!'

Merko cast a vicious glance into space. 'They laughed at me,' he said. 'Now they're sniveling because I put them out of business. They sneak around after my secret. They'd kiss me anywhere. I made one of them – I hate people touching me, so I made him do it, for the 'secret,' and then I told him: "Throw yourself off a mountain."'

Merko's eyes glowed in the serene afternoon. Hal felt that his eyes were glowing too, and suddenly he grew frightened. He was talking to an illegal person who might lead him to a precipice, to crash on rocks he wasn't ready for. Yet when Merko leaped to his feet, he leaped too, and went running after his maniacal brother in greater fear that he might lose him.

Merko pointed. 'There's my place.'

Hal saw a tiny cottage on top of the next hill. It appeared to be surrounded by a motionless slide of rocks, except that the avalanche – beginning as it did at the hill-top – couldn't have come from anywhere. They turned into a grove of pine trees, and it was surprising to come upon a small cabin there. A golden-headed little girl about five years old was playing with pine cones in the front yard, and she called out happily: 'Hi, Uncle Merko!'

'Hello, youngster,' Merko responded gruffly, without looking at her.

'I like little girls,' said Hal.

'They're better than the grown-up kind.'

Hal realized that he hadn't connected Merko with a girl, a wife, or anyone. Merko spat. 'Women are no good in my business,' he muttered, and quickly ran ahead. Hal was used to the maneuver now. He could tell when he had embarrassed Merko, for it was at these times that he abruptly changed his pace or tone. Whenever he spat, it marked the punctuation of his mood.

'Women drag you down!'

'Well . . .'

'I don't need them. I don't like effeminate people hanging around me anyway. They can't climb. What can they do? Trap you! Make sure you keep your *rubbers on*,' Merko emphasized with a revolting leer. They tramped through more pine cones, and he kicked at them.

'Who lives back there?' Hal asked, as they started up the hill.

'Someone I used to know.'

'The little girl seems to – '

'Girl!' said Merko angrily. 'He's got three more inside.'

'Don't you like them?'

'I bring them candy. What am I supposed to do? They can't help all the ruin they cause.'

Hal gasped as he came up against Merko's pointed elbow.

'You can come along to my place – if you want to,' Merko sneered. 'As long as you're here.' He seemed lost in a furious embarrassment. 'What do I care? You don't have to come – I'll tell you one thing, I'm not going to buy any life insurance, if that's what you're looking for. You think you can *agree* me into doing anything you want, but it won't work. Do you know something? I don't even like you.'

It was time not to agree.

'I can make you like me,' Hal said calmly.

'Come on,' Merko said. 'Watch out for the rocks.'

They trudged up the hill past loose stones and boulders on all sides that seemed ready to topple if they were breathed upon.

19

Merko

They sat down to dinner at half past four, and the whole business – the hour, the dinner, the house and furniture, and what they said to one another – was all out of kilter. Merko opened the blinds, letting in a flood of sunlight that seemed to become hotter as it grew later, yet he sat in it wearing a dark coat, and frowned when Hal opened his collar.

They had grapes and walnuts and a kind of sour cream. Then Merko heated up a can of corned-beef hash. This was followed by lobster claws and apple pie, and finally a slice of hot rare roast beef. Now that dinner was over, Merko was chewing gum and mixing martinis in a huge cocktail-shaker. He shook the silver vessel so hard, with such minute vibrations, that it did not appear to move in his small, bony hands.

It was the second round. Merko was already quite drunk. He shouted: 'We're having what is known as *a good time*!' He roared with laughter at the slightest provocation. Thrusting the cocktail-shaker under Hal's nose, still vibrating it, he chuckled. '*Here's* what'll make us friendly. That's the idea, isn't it?'

Hal's stomach was in a turmoil. He had been afraid to refuse the mélange of courses, but he needed will power like Merko's to keep them down. Every new serving that went into his stomach immediately revolted against the course that preceded it. He felt his stomach beginning very slowly to turn over. On the phonograph Merko was playing what sounded like Arabian music . . .

And it was not only what was going on inside of him, but what he looked at. Every object in Merko's house, and in his life, was systematically placed to violate every other object. Anyone taking inventory when the owner was not around would have found it impossible to tell what kind of person lived here.

There was a set of bar bells and some half-finished embroidery on a lace napkin; on one table copies of *Vogue* and *Boxing &*

Wrestling magazines. Around the walls hung reproductions of a severe Madonna, a calendar girl on a tiger-skin rug, Degas dancers, a canvas crowded with red-coated huntsmen drinking beer, another girl (February) crouched naked on skis, an actual American flag crossed with the flag of British Honduras, a map of Nantucket, and above the front door, where a tuxedo hung down the length of peeling logs, the head and shoulders of someone with a small, indistinct face being crucified.

Again, in the bookcase a chaos of titles and authors had obviously been arranged to destroy one another: *A Laugh a Day Keeps the Doctor Away*, *The Divine Comedy*, *Stover at Yale*, *Apologia Pro Vita Sua*, *You Are What You Eat*, *Plays of Lope de Vega*, *Art of the Pole Vault*, *Black Beauty*, *Macbeth*, *Away to the Gaspé*; Woodford, Browning, Jonathan Edwards, Baudelaire, Louisa May Alcott; and after the startling homogeneity of three idlers, Walton, Pepys, and Omar Khayyam, two books in the right corner of the bottom shelf bound in heavy black tape, *Prometheus Unbound* and *The World as Will and Idea*.

Yet, perversely, on the table adjacent to these two God-challenging volumes were the remains of a game of solitaire swept away, some of it fallen to the floor. All about the room there were similar signs of idleness, doodles on odd pieces of paper, completed crossword puzzles, a page of chess problems, and on one sheet an infinity of tic-tac-toes going off the edge of the paper, as if the player had gone mad trying to beat himself.

But among these remnants of fanatic time-wasting could be seen the evidence of desperate stretches of labor, of mind and conscience – the proposition typed out:

Achilles pursues the tortoise. During the split second he draws exactly even, the tortoise moves a little bit ahead. Since at the one instant of evenness the tortoise will always be moving forward, no matter how fast Achilles runs he is unable logically to pass the crawling animal.

And below hammered out in black capitals: 'DISPROVE THIS.'
Piles of crushed paper surrounded the typewriter. Elsewhere, amid more crumpled sheets, Hal glimpsed the fragment:

> Blasted by Bright Agonies of the Mind,
> O, Neighbors, Neighbors, think me not unkind . . .

117

Near by lay a little prayer book with a knotted ribbon smeared in mud.

Merko was walking around, brandishing the shaker and shouting to Hal: 'Drink up! Come on, you want to make friends with me, don't you?'

Hal drained his glass and held it out for more. He was no longer feeling sick. He felt himself floating on top of a tremendous martini.

'Have some more, you phony! Drink up, or I'll force it down your gozzle!'

Hal had one. Although the gin mists were rising around the edges of his mind, he saw through them coolly. He knew that Merko was disturbed that he hadn't been able to frighten him, and now he was putting on more wild behavior to drive him away. Merko had some terrible weakness to hide. But he would give it away to the Young Man Like Everybody Else from whom no secret could be kept.

'You can't *yes* me, god damn it.' Merko tilted the shaker to his lips and swallowed everything in it. He stood before Hal, weaving, with a bumptious grin. 'Mr Life-Insurance Man . . .

'Phony!' exclaimed Merko, with incomprehensible delight that this should be so. 'You're nothing but a hat rack. You haven't got any character at all. You aren't anybody – just a hat hanging on nothing. Get up. You can't sit there. Go stand by the door where you belong.'

He actually made a motion to pull Hal out of the chair, but was halted by a long sad smile.

'Don't give me that smirk. You don't know anything.'

Hal hadn't in fact any reason for smiling, except to seem mysterious and thereby distract Merko from laying hands on him. It was the right thing to do. Merko stepped back. He made a desperate gesture with both hands, and the cocktail-shaker fell to the floor.

'Don't you pretend to feel sorry for me!' he shouted.

But Hal was saying gently: 'You poor guy. I'll bet you haven't got a friend in the world. Why don't you let yourself go, and be like other people?'

With a roar of self-pity Merko sat down on the floor and began rocking with his head in his hands. Then, as Hal expected, Merko told him his life story.

20
The Life of an Individualist

The Flying Merkos. They didn't want the baby. Tried everything, but they couldn't stop it. Knew it would wreck the act, so she lay all day long in hot baths, ate horse pills, and fell downstairs. An indomitable little creature kept growing inside her. At night she felt drums in her abdomen, feet and fists hammering, wanting out. After a while she began to giggle. 'Thad,' she said, 'it'll be a strong one.' He only grunted. 'What's going to happen to me – without a partner?' he demanded. She let him put her over a barrel a few more times, but then she wouldn't. They had to make the best of the situation. 'Hey,' he said one night, 'I got it.' He told her. At first she wasn't sure. 'Whatsa matter?' She couldn't say. She kissed him, and they lay in bed making plans. The act would be greater than ever, after all, and they dreamed of the Biggest Top . . .

'SHE FLIES THROUGH THE AIR WITH HER BABY ON HER BACK.' He had come out, and they started using him when he was four months old. The first agent they showed it to almost went crazy – booked them in every state. There weren't any laws against it, because nobody had ever tried such a thing before. No violation of child labor either. All he did was lie there in the papoose arrangement strapped onto her shoulders. They taught him to smile and how to fall (which babies know pretty well anyway) and, after a few months, to smile *while* he was falling . . .

These were his earliest memories: the muscles of his mother's back straining under him; diving out of great dark theaters into a blazing light full of ropes and rings; his old man, now far away and suddenly swooping toward him, the tensing of his mother's flanks, a flip, ropes, wires, burning hoop, and pale sweaty arms around him; or falling, falling until he finally hit a net and rebounded, smiling at a roar of faces . . .

I was born into an unnatural act. It was what shocked people – and

119

brought in the money. Whatever town they played, as soon as the posters went up, some church or women's club would complain. But they would have warned the manager beforehand – wait, wait, just one show. They knew. The people who came to cry shame on her always ended up yelling for joy at this wonderful mother-son relationship . . .

He grew older. The posters had to be changed. 'SHE FLIES THROUGH THE AIR WITH HER BOY ON HER BACK.' He began to get embarrassed by the blown-up photos in the lobby.

The old man was getting moody. *I couldn't help it.* He was sore because he didn't count any more, with the crowds, with her. Nobody wanted to watch him do nipups. The kid was the thing. The woman and the kid. And they were getting pretty close together lately, leaving him out of the conversation. Soon he was sulking all the time. Up on the trapeze his sweaty face gazed at them mournfully. A couple of performances he didn't show up and it made no difference. The agent told him he might as well stay out of the act altogether. He hung around.

What was I supposed to do? One night mother and son missed the rings and fell into the net together. There was a long agonized shout as they went down, but to show they weren't hurt the mother lifted up her boy in her arms and kissed him and *presented* him, arms outstretched to the audience; he smiling, of course, out of habit or rather necessity (his mouth automatically opened and drew into a curve when they were in mid-air) and the crowd cried and blew kisses at them. After that she insisted on using the fake fall and kiss as a socko finale.

He was sick of it. Never had a chance to be alone, to be *himself.* They were always following him around, the old lady with love, the old man with advice. The old man kept whining and complaining: 'It's time you went out on your own. Stand on your own feet. You're getting to be a burden on your mother.'

The two things he hated most in the world – love and advice. If they had left him alone long enough, he could have got set and orphaned his mind, but he had no self to operate from. He tried to look himself up in libraries, in the eyes of his schoolmates (he changed schools at least three times a year), in what his schoolteachers said. No answer had been created to fit him. The schoolboys thought he was strange for riding on his mother's back. The teachers considered him strange for asking if he couldn't come and live with them. The library books (all of which seemed to have been written for parents) told him only that he was maladjusted. *Bastards!* One time he skipped his gym workout and ran into a church. 'Honor thy father and mother,' said the man in charge, looking at him strangely.

He was a thankless son. He didn't appreciate all the pain and heart-strain she was going through on his account. The old man kept beating on him: 'You ought to be ashamed. It's time you worked up an act of your own.' She flared up: 'What kind of a father are you? What are you wishing on the little boy?' 'I'm taking over,' the old man said. 'The boy's coming up aloft with me for some solo training.' But he himself was trembling. He bungled the first catch and they fell. With a shriek she swung the net under where her son was falling. The old man hit the floor on his head. *I couldn't help it!*

It knocked the old man queer. He lost all interest in life except to break up the mother-and-son act which he (he forgot) had created in the first place. Wandering and murmuring to himself, he followed them from theater to theater crying out against woman's folly and his son's unmanliness. He reinforced his lamentations with horoscopes and statistics – charts of performance curves, aging curves, and cycles of fortune proving that the day had nearly come when they were bound to slip. They tried to drive him away, but he hung around.

The old man had to be right, of course. One day or another. Three months past his fifteenth birthday the boy felt her body groan under him, and they fell. He found the net, but she landed exactly as the old man had . . .

The world blamed me! The old man told all the papers: 'He made her do it. He had a hold over her and wouldn't let go!' 'My little boy!' she moaned at the hospital. 'My broken-headed little boy.' It was useless to point out to her that she was the one with the fractured skull. For the rest of her life she refused to believe this.

Somebody got out an injunction against me. Facing the music, he scuffed his toe on the floor, and the judge said: 'We have bred a vicious generation.' 'Farp,' he thought, 'farp.' 'But thank God in this case . . . it's not too late . . . paraphrase Victor Hugo . . . stands in the docket with every young delinquent . . . depravity not born but . . . in a sense each of us personally responsible . . . society . . . High hopes . . . dismissed.' Paroled to his parents, in psychiatric custody.

. . . 'Look, son, you seem determined to make yourself into a very unhappy young man. But what for? There's no sense in it. I'm speaking from your own point of view. Let's suppose all your resentments are perfectly justified. Well, so what? Nursing the grudge will only make you unhappier. And in spite of your pose to the contrary, I know you don't want to be unhappy. At bottom you're a social animal like the rest of us.' *'I am myself.'* 'True enough. You've said that many times. But one is more than oneself. One is a member – ' *'Farp.'* 'You see! There's the pattern of resentment emerging again.' *'Farp.'* 'The irony of it, boy, is that you're trying so desperately to be different – yet really your problems are exactly the same as those of hundreds of other boys I've talked to. The same tone, same reactions, same words even – and the same will to be miserable. Don't you want to be happy?' *'I want to be myself.'* 'Yes, I know. Frankly, I would have to be a complete idiot not to be aware of this desire in you by now. But here's another approach. Have you ever heard of the poet John Donne? He was a very wise fellow. He said: "No man" – it applies equally to boys – "No man is an island . . ."' *'Farp.'*

Eighteen. The day of freedom. The old man wanted him to settle for the trapeze. 'It's a safe and steady living.' 'Always work over a net!' she cried, snuffling interminable good-bys. He ran out of the house. One thing he knew. He was made for something better than the trapeze. He didn't want merely to earn a living. He wanted to *express himself.* How, God knew. He got on a train, shivering, crying to himself at the enormous discrepancy between his aims and abilities.

Runaway. Roustabout. Years of misery. Tugging resentfully on ropes, hoisting aloft circus girls whose petty antics disgusted him in comparison with what his mother used to do, and then *that* disgusted him, and he'd shut his eyes so hard there were circles of light in them, and pull, and haul, and he'd only watch the men. Yet he despised them too, for their arrogant display of picture muscle, and the skill they had in performing trivial tricks – routines laid out long ago by others, irrelevant, uncreative, challenging nothing. He knew he could do better, *the best,* if he could be alone in the tent some night, all to himself. Alone he would go flying through hot, silent, klieg-lighted spaces. Gradually as the hours went by he would discover the unperformed twists, flings, and leaps that were now imprisoned in his body. Ultimately there would come the one leap. It would express him absolutely, and therefore at its climax violate some law of nature.

But he never had this chance to be alone. His body was in the service of others. There was no pause in life. A man was picked up in the tempo of this life, and couldn't get off it. The body had no time to reflect. It spent its energies working for other bodies. It developed co-operative reflexes instead of expressive ones. Eventually your body didn't dare ... They were always after him, hurrying, imposing on his body. Not just the job, the girls. They teased him beyond endurance.

I swore I'd never touch a woman, and I never have. He fought off their soft ways. Took long cold showers. When they pawed at him he ran from them. Swarming up ropes pursued by laughing circus girls. One day the boss caught sight of him in wild flight through the rigging, and was astonished. 'Hey, we can use that!' Later, on the ground, observing the crab-apple muscles of his discovery's arms and legs, he shook his head. 'You can't make it in tights.' But then he brightened. 'So who wants you in tights? You're a natural comic! We'll do it just like I saw you. Putty up your nose and have the girls chase you, and then they catch up with you, see, and ...'

I quit. No women were going to handle him. The idea of a woman's hand touching him was enough to make him tremble. The threat of clinging bodies made him want to *soar* free – running wasn't fast enough. Threats of soft flesh entered his dreams. Their bodies hunted him night after night. Yet even in his sleep he managed to thwart them by waking up on the instant and rushing for the cold shower, and he had never lost this race. If possible, the dreams of muscular flesh were even worse, for they always turned into his old lady, and he was transported back into vaudeville, once more the little jockey. Either they didn't measure up to her, or they were too much like her. And now, quitting, he stayed true to himself ...

The Depression. Window-washer. Steeple jack. Gym teacher in a boys' prep school. Clerk of the body. High diver. Flagpole-sitter gaping at the sky. The servant of others. Walkathon – pulled a tendon; the Boston Marathon – flopped in the Newton hills. Years. Desperation. He was no nearer to expressing himself, and time was passing. *Was* he like all the others? Born to be humbled, hobbled? ... *Bastards!* He gritted his teeth. Six-day bicycle race. Came in last. Rodeo. A humped-back Brahma bull – volunteers – ride him for just ten seconds. A thousand dollars. 'Can You Ride Big Sam?' He couldn't. Acrobat, ventriloquist, a gloomy song and dance. Fired. Knockabout stooge for three Turkish weight-lifters. Let a magician pull yards of flannel out of his nose. Slack wire, teeterboard, trampoline. Finally with suction cups on his shoes, now at the point where the only way he could make a living was by walking upside down.

Hanging upside down, thinking. He took a step. A cymbal crashed in the orchestra pit. Another step. Crash. A child howled out of the balcony. The sound infuriated him. All at once he saw the ridiculousness of his position. 'What am I doing here?' He would have thrown his arms in the air, but they were already dangling down, so he could only crook his elbows, clench his fists, and once more plant his foot on the aboveboard to the accompaniment of the cymbal. 'WHAT AM I DOING HERE?' 'Mama!' cried the child in the balcony. 'When's he supposed to fall?' He swayed a moment.

'Now, youngster!' he bellowed. Wrenching one foot free and then the other, he fell twirling in one, two somersaults. *I landed on my feet.* He thumbed his nose at all the world he could see, and, followed by a chorus of boos, rushed offstage.

Later, laughter followed him into the cool alley behind the theater. He had expected this, and distributed bloody noses among them. But so ridiculous did he appear that the wire-walkers and acrobats had gone on laughing anyway, bloody noses and all.

Let them. *I'd whip gravity.* It was no wild impulse. He had been mulling it over for days before the answer hit him. It was simple. WILL POWER.

Leaving the laughter of oafs behind him, he made for the high ledge he'd had in mind for so long. He went straight to his objective. Exactly straight. That was the idea. No physical object would be permitted to detour him. He would make no concessions. Whatever was in his way he would knock down, climb, or jump over, but *make*. Because it was his will to do so. He would just GO.

Bound for the mountain, splashing across moonlit brooks. Unless they coincided with his path, bridges did not exist. (Up and over a haystack.) Punish yourself, whip yourself, but make it. For nothing. For absolutely no reason except that he felt like it. Or perhaps because he didn't feel like it at all, and would therefore exercise his will in the opposite direction. (Through a field of thistles.) Simply force his body to do whatever he ordered, or else. *One slip and you're through.* He could, if he chose, eat a rock. If it got stuck he would sit down and systematically knead it through his intestines, and go on. For nothing. He felt a great wind of freedom blowing on him. It hummed through the barbed-wire fences. (Climbing a house, shots in the night. 'Thief!') March on, he said.

It seemed to him that his will had become a huge new muscle within his body, invisible to others, but huge, exerting irresistible leverage on all his other muscles.

(After the prickly hedge, a crown of thorns. Up the mountain now, thrashing steadily uphill through tangles of scrub.) He spat at a near-by star. Not out of malice. He just couldn't hold himself in. Alone for the first time in his life. Himself. Emancipated from the very earth.

There was no feat of any description that he couldn't accomplish once he put his mind to it. Not part or most of his mind, but absolutely all of it. Which meant cutting free of everybody, every consideration in the world but the one objective. Go blind except for one tiny gimlet hole of fixed intent, and then go. No one had ever gone the way he knew how to go. Because they had cared a little bit, paused, considered, thought about consequences. Even the ruthless ones were wary. *They didn't carry it all the way.*

But he would now free himself of the last laws and limitations of man, and (say, precisely because he didn't want to) break them one by one – gravity, decency, diminishing returns, conservation of energy. Ignore space and time, and, to do this, break free of habit. Have no habits. Seeing life as a whirling disk and all men in their grooves, he would be a needle dragging back and forth across the record, expressing nothing but his own will perhaps, but *making his own sound*, he would go.

Give him an obstacle, any damned circumstance or thing, and he would hit it head on, billygoat it, and ram and batter, and crowd, push, unload on it, scrabble, reach, claw, and keep on fighting not merely to the death but through death and out the other side to life again, and keep on, and again, until he couldn't go any further, and still go on, extending himself to the last thread of the last fiber of muscle he possessed, and then shred that last thread infinitely until he had it (for no special reason) made.

Bursting out of the last patch of scrub, he reached the top of the mountain. He went out on the ledge and sat there until the sunrise revealed the pink rocks at the bottom of the precipice. 'Go ahead,' the voice said, 'let's see if you can do it.' He listened for a while to the voice telling him that he would not be killed. The sun grew brighter. The rocks turned yellow, and then became clear, of no color; he saw all their points and edges. *It.* He went over with a shout of joy.

'But you're alive,' murmured Hal, who had almost fallen asleep.

'It was a hundred feet down,' said Merko, 'with those rocks at the bottom. But something told me: 'You won't be killed because *you will not.*' In the air it was my last thought: *'You will not.'*

'I came down smash. After a while I heard a voice crying – me, of course – and I knew I had made it because there was my body sort of strewn all around me, *destroyed*, except that I *wouldn't* be. I began laughing at my body because it couldn't endure the pain, but it had to. I told my cowardly body: 'You see, I mean business. Let's go now.'

'I crawled home!' cried the little man. 'That was the test. And when I got there I made myself a cup of tea because I didn't want it. I drank it very slowly before I crawled down to the main road. Then a fellow came along in a car and I *refused* him – to teach my body another lesson, and when the second car came I was making for another cliff. You know why I let that one take me to the hospital?'

'What does he want me to say?' Hal wondered dazedly, as he shrank from Merko's sawing arms.

'Because by that time you'd already proved – '

'Pure caprice!' said his host in a nearly inaudible whisper, and fell lolling into an armchair.

His Adam's apple moved in long convulsions. He appeared not so much drunk as exhausted. His eyelids were red, his cheeks white and sunken, and all at once he was a used-up little man, a possible candidate for life insurance.

He got up again and moved about the room, and now he was puttering, touching his caprices. He picked up a crossword puzzle, scribbled in a few letters, and put it down. He applied a brown crayon to a sketch of several frolicking horses; rattled out a sentence on his typewriter; took a desultory bang at the punching-bag.

'It's all a hoax!' he muttered.

'What?'

'This life,' said Merko, and he toppled with a gentle sigh face down on the rug.

'Oh, well,' thought Hal woozily. 'It's the only one we've got. Might as well make the best . . .'

The room began whirling around him faster and faster. He lay down carefully by Merko's side, and let drunkenness in, and sleep.

21

Hal and Merko

Hal woke up to a bright morning. The air was sweet and fresh. A loud twittering was in progress. Hundreds of birds were hopping among the boulders, and he saw that Merko was feeding them. The little man made funny clucking sounds. He seemed to be talking to his guests. Hal sank back onto the bed, and realized that Merko must have carried him into the room. He remembered nothing of it. His eyes felt sunken in and his tongue was furry. Someone had filled his head with cement.

Merko returned to the kitchen and began making scrambled eggs and bacon. The smell of the bacon was delicious. Merko leaned in the bedroom doorway and shouted jovially: 'Big party, eh! Come on and have some breakfast.'

Hal washed his face, and without thinking anything of it borrowed Merko's razor. It occurred to him that he had left his tennis racket and overnight bag at the Olympic Club. The hotel people were probably thinking that he had skipped. Perhaps they had impounded his clothes. It didn't matter. He had a strange, free feeling of being on a holiday. He splashed on some of Merko's shaving lotion, and yelped with pain. It had obviously been made to test the man who used it. The lotion seemed to put flames to his skin, yet as soon as he came into the kitchen he had a pulsing, happy face, and he was starting to feel fine.

'Drink up,' Merko commanded.

Hal found that he was confronted with a cold, black, glistening bottle of beer, and that he was laughing and drinking at this wrong time of day. Beer for breakfast, it turned out, was just the thing. He had another bottle with his scrambled eggs. Merko washed the dishes and went outside, and Hal realized that they had not spoken since he sat down to breakfast. Yet their silence had not been strained. All tension between them had disappeared, as if during the time they slept they had unconsciously become friends.

He went outdoors, expecting to find Merko, but his host was nowhere to be seen. He walked about the hilltop, among the boulders. The birds were gone. It was absolutely quiet. The faintest of breezes played over the arrested landslide. He felt a marvelous clarity in the day. He was not afraid of life here, because there was only Merko. There was no need to adjust to him, and besides it was impossible. How could he centralize himself to a madman who had broken away from the very reflexes of mankind and set up his own nervous system?

He thought: 'Should I try to imitate him?' It was against nature. He and Merko were brothers in their oppositeness. Perhaps each had found the only friend he could possibly have. The one Just Like Everybody Else and the other Like Nobody Else were in perfect equilibrium. Now he would make no attempt to centralize Merko, who in turn would not use will power on him, and they would have a few hours on a hilltop until, for no reason, they went their separate ways.

He heard shouts below. They were childish voices, and he remembered the little girl they had passed in front of the cabin. Presently he saw what looked like the back of an elephant bobbing up the hill. It was the sack full of coins, with Merko gritting his teeth under it. Merko flung his load among the rocks. His crimson face was expressionless. He was determined not to breathe hard after his climb, and avoided this weakness, Hal saw, by refusing for the moment to breathe at all.

They sat down on the cobblestoned terrace, drinking again. Merko still kept on his head the handkerchief rolled into a sort of turban he had worn during his climb. He reminded Hal, despite the menial headpiece, of a sahib, perhaps because he drank his gin and lemon juice with an elegant air and said rather precisely: 'I like you better today. You have a face.'

'What did I have yesterday?' Hal laughed.

'Nothing! Just a blank space. That's because you agree with everybody. Don't think I didn't see you in town, when they were throwing money at me. I looked around the crowd, and I saw this empty area under a hat. It was your face, but there was nothing in it. Do you know that? Do you know what's going to happen to you?'

'I'll be happy, Merko.'

The little man laughed, and drank some more gin.

'Well, what is going to happen to me?' Hal asked, annoyed by this attitude.

Merko shook his head. 'I won't tell you.'

'You'll never be happy, Merko.'

'I spit on happiness. I rise above it!' said Merko, obviously not doing so. He tried to speak haughtily from his deck chair, but remained a lonely little fellow in a turban.

'You're just like that girl,' Hal said.

'What *girl?*'

'The one I met yesterday at the Olympic Club. You're both too proud. You won't give in to anything, and so you're miserable.'

'What won't a girl give into?'

Hal told him about Joan Vigoro. As soon as he mentioned that she was a high-jumper, Merko put down his glass of gin and listened closely. 'They didn't want her to run fast, eh?' he chuckled. He scowled on hearing that all the athletes had turned their backs on her, and disagreed fiercely when Hal denounced her stubbornness.

'What do you mean!' he interrupted. 'Now there's a girl – '

'Yes, but look what it's done to her. She's given up everything, and she's going to be the mail-order bride of an old man.'

'What!' shouted Merko, leaping from his chair. 'Well, then, she's weak. Otherwise she wouldn't do that. I knew it!' He picked up his gin glass and flung it into the valley.

But later he suggested: 'When you go back to town, I'll help you sell some insurance to those people over at that Olympic Club you were talking about.' It would be on his way, Merko explained, because this evening he was going to see about performing on an upraised drawbridge in East Riverton.

They started off down the hill to the place where Merko left his motorcycle. There was no sound from the cabin surrounded with pine cones where they had met the little girl. Some distance across the meadow Hal caught sight of a group of people struggling toward them.

'There he is,' said Merko. 'Now you'll see what I mean.'

The approaching unit was a family – father, mother, and four children.

'Don't speak to 'em. Just keep going,' Merko growled.

The man and wife walked hand in hand. She was gazing up at

him adoringly. He could hardly keep up with her because the children were climbing all over him. Hal recognized the little girl of the day before wrapped around her father's leg. Two equally golden-headed creatures dragged at his arms. Another swung on his neck. He hobbled along, with only one leg free. Rearing above the tender, clinging bodies, he was huge and lithe. His hair was black, and he had a magnificent corded neck. At one time he must have had a romantic hawk face but now it had gone somewhat to flesh. His eyes were weary. He saw Merko, and made a noticeable attempt to straighten up. But the children, apparently sensing his effort, bore down harder on him with merry shouts.

He began smiling apologetically, from yards away. His little blonde wife gave Merko a look of entreaty. But Merko gave them nothing. He wouldn't look at them.

'Hi, Uncle Merko, where you goin'?' called his tiny girl friend, and he answered, scowling: 'To Riverton, youngster,' and passed them without breaking stride.

'Who is that?' Hal asked.

'Laocoön!' Merko laughed harshly. 'Laocoön Smith.'

'That's a peculiar name.'

'His name is Dudley. He used to climb with me.'

'He looks as if he wanted you to forgive him for something.'

'Of course he does,' said Merko, 'but I won't forgive him. What's the good of it? You can't change history. He didn't measure up, that's all, and he and I both know it. I could forgive him until I was black in the face, and the historical fact still would be that he went soft and left me, and broke up our act.'

'Why did he go soft?'

'As you see.'

'Well . . .' Hal looked back. 'I see he's got a beautiful wife there, and four – '

'A ruined man,' said Merko. 'Fat-assed, entwined in children. That's all that's left of him now. But you should have seen him when he first came to me.'

Merko spat on the grass. Dudley Smith, he said. A young gymnast just out of college, he had seen Merko aloft one afternoon and come to him, begging to be apprenticed. He felt that there was more to life than swinging on parallel bars.

In the classic manner of the master vis-à-vis the neophyte, Merko was dour and discouraging: 'It's tough, thankless *practice* . . .

months of slaving in a gym . . . unlearn everything you ever knew.' But the boy insisted. Merko took him on, proudly watched him develop, never gave him a word of praise. Only when he remained silent was he satisfied.

Eventually they made a great team, did hand-balancing acts from mile-high cornices. Young Smith became the idol of high-school and college girls in every public square. Merko knew this was poison, and warned his protégé that women were the enemies of all dedicated men. The boy pretended to agree, but 'I could see his eyes wandering.' One day Merko came upon him in a drugstore booth. A fragile little blonde was stroking his hair and talking earnestly to him.

That afternoon they were to dangle from some gargoyles. The boy faltered. His teeth were chattering. A gale was blowing on them, all the better for swinging, but the boy stared at a tiny blond head far below. 'It's too wi-windy!' he stammerd. 'Quit if you want to,' Merko said, and scornfully watched him crawl down. When he was near the ground, Merko tossed a fluttering white handkerchief after him, and – although they had places on the same hillside near Riverton – never spoke to him again. 'Now he's a building-inspector,' Merko said to Hal. 'Imagine it. He checks buildings for safety. They come up here on their days off to try and make up with me, but I'll never let them!'

'You blame her?' asked Hal, feeling sorry for Laocoön Smith.

'Well, it wasn't her fault. She was born a weak woman and couldn't change. It was his lookout. He got what he deserved, all right. There was a softness in him. He didn't really want to climb. He picked a weak and clinging woman because he had to have delicacy,' Merko said in a mincing tone, indicating this quality with his thumb and forefinger.

'It's too bad she came along.'

'Somebody else would have. Besides, history isn't interested in excuses why a building isn't climbed. If you don't make it, you don't, and it's your fault. *Yours*,' Merko emphasized. 'A stomach-ache is your fault. If a manhole cover blows off, sails up ten stories, and decapitates you in an elevator, it's your fault.'

'You know, a man could still climb,' Hal thought aloud, 'if his wife left him alone – if she knew how to take care of herself.'

'A strong one,' Merko agreed enthusiastically. Then his face darkened. He was thinking of his mother.

Hal said: 'I mean a girl who's different – more like a companion.'

'That's it! A real companion. You know, *clean*. None of this . . .' Merko groaned. 'If I had the luck to meet someone who didn't want the *soft side* of love.' He gave Hal a wild, questioning stare. 'Hey? Can you imagine a girl like that? Can you?'

'They say there's a girl for everybody,' Hal answered, as they reached the motorcycle.

On the way back to town the landscape and the day seemed to grow softer in outline. Hal's thoughts became softer and less distinct. He replied to Merko with remote smiles. Merko and his problems lost importance, now that they were returning to the world. The main thing, he thought happily and indifferently, was to pick up his belongings and catch the bus for Boston.

Merko's arrival made a sensation at the Riverton Olympic Club. Tim Ashburn was not there, but Big Dick Trent, Fred Watt, and the others wanted an introduction to 'the guy who licked Lumpy Modoc.' They surrounded him with worshipful questions. How did he train? Did he have a special diet? Soft-legged girls in shorts pressed on him admiringly. To all of them he muttered: 'Pleased to meetchu,' and rammed his hands deeper in his pockets. He made a fierce, pleading sign to Hal, who pointed to the high-jumping pit.

At that moment Joan Vigoro with her long legs outflung went soaring over the bar, and Merko, gazing over the heads of the athletes, gasped and turned pale. She arose from the soft earth, her dark, sorrowful countenance quickly turned away from the crowd, and returned to her take-off point. There she hung her head, and seemed to be musing on the end of her life, but suddenly gathered her strength and ran and jumped again in a desperately unhappy flight over the long stick of balsa wood.

Merko started walking toward her like a zombi. The crowd of athletes respectfully stepped aside, as did Hal, to see what would happen. But nothing happened. The two simply stared at one another, like two children meeting for the first time in the park. Merko flexed his hands. The bitter, shamefaced girl refused him the slightest greeting. Yet they couldn't go away from each other either. Seeing this, Hal ran up and introduced them. They clasped hands and backed off again.

Hal started to leave them, but Merko clutched him saying: 'No!'

'What's the matter?'

Slowly Joan Vigoro turned away and went back to the jumping-pit.

'What's the matter with you?'

'I can't! Not yet. She's clean all right, but I've got to take my time. Stick with me!' Merko whispered.

'You'd better hurry. Remember, she's a mail-order bride,' said Hal.

'Stick with me!'

'I'm going to get my stuff, and then check out of the hotel.'

'Why?' demanded Merko, trembling as Joan went over the bar again.

'I've got to get back to Boston,' Hal said. He didn't know why, except that it was the appropriate thing to do. He had a fiancée there and a business. He lived at the Circle Hotel. And now that they had come down from the hilltop, Merko seemed just like any other unimportant human being – especially since the sight of a girl had made him lose his power.

'When are you coming back?'

He might need to go up on the hilltop again. 'Soon,' Hal promised. 'Maybe in a month or so.'

'We're pals!'

'Right. Keep after her now.'

They were engulfed in athletes again, and Hal slipped away. Before reaching the clubhouse, he heard a harsh voice explaining to the crowd: 'Punish yourself! Whip yourself! One slip and you're through!'

22

July in Boston

Boston Common was a meadow full of pretty girls offering themselves to the sun. The great medicine ball was blazing away everybody's imperfections. Now and then a broad belt of wind moved across the field. The shape of each gust could be followed by lines of bright fluttering dresses and tumbled hair. In a rippling pattern, dozens of small white arms came up to smooth and pat the hair. Meanwhile the wind hit some underbrush, rushed through the trees, kicked up dust on the far baseball diamond, and then had not, it seemed, ever existed, except that the sun felt a bit hotter than before.

The few men on the Common were a drab breed. There was something of the barnyard about them. Their shirts were stained. The sleeves flapped on their forearms. Rose wasn't afraid of them, as she used to be. Rather she felt sorry for them because they were so unattractive. She herself had changed. Soon her boy with the slanted hat would be home.

The last Hal had seen of her (since, after it was over in the room, they had kept the lights off) she had been a pinched little stick of a girl, anxious and ugly. Now, although she still weighed one hundred and twelve, she didn't feel thin any more. There was a more womanly tint to her flesh. Her arms were no longer pale and bony, but delicately tanned and fuller and softer. He would be amazed at the improvement.

There was a burst of melody near by, and a trembling tenor voice sang out of violins: 'The very birds do cry!' She arched her back, leaning on her braced arms. Then she became aware of the tentative boy ambling around her in circles with a self-conscious smile, drawing a bit closer with each circuit he made. He carried a portable radio. Nodding to her, he turned the volume down.

He was a slight, weak-looking boy with a long face and comically hollow eyes. His straw-colored hair stuck up in spikes, evidence of the desperate applications of vaseline that had kept it in place in front of the mirror – only to have it spring up again after he had taken two or three steps. A brown sport shirt revealed his feeble, freckled arms. On the most beautiful day in July his face was pale and shiny and sad, and he said: 'I've seen you around.'

This forlorn confidence made her laugh. Out of habit she was about to snap back: 'Well, isn't that a thrill,' when she remembered that she didn't have to be sarcastic any more.

'I've been watching you,' the boy stated. The radio in his hand was still going. The announcer said faintly: 'Now Art Christian wants to know "How High the Moon?"' before he was switched off.

'I even know your name,' the boy continued in a humble sing-song, in which there was also a note of yokel pride. 'Your name is Rose. You know how I know it? I stood under your window – I mean, your office window. I work in the same building you do, did you know that? In the clinic. I sweep the floors. I heard him call you Rose.'

She looked at this adolescent who had waited under her window, not sure whether to be angry or touched, or perhaps a bit worried. Finally she decided not to care, and to be gentle with him.

'I never thought I'd get up the nerve to speak to you,' he said.

'Well, it's perfectly all right,' she answered. 'It's very nice, but I don't think you'd better – '

'Why not?' said the boy earnestly. 'What I mean, us lonely people ought to get together.'

'What!' cried Rose. 'Who's lonely? What do you mean by saying that? My fiancé is coming back next week.' This was so humiliating. Her feeling of grace and prettiness vanished. All mercy gone, she stormed at him: 'Go away! Get away from here.'

He stared at her, pathetic and round-eyed, unaware that he had committed the greatest slander, and mumbled: 'Gee, I didn't know.'

'And you had better try to take better care of your appearance,' she said coldly, realizing that he had done the best he could to no avail. She added half-heartedly: 'Look at your shoes.'

At this the boy stumbled away. His grief-stricken manner appalled her. She had never really hurt anyone like this. She called after him: 'Wait!' But he would not. She followed after him, saying: 'Please!'

'You'll never see me again,' he said. As she tried once more to say she was sorry, the radio roared out Art Christian's arrangement of 'Poor Little Buttercup.'

On the way back to her office Rose stopped and gazed unbelievingly at someone on the corner of Charles and Beacon. 'It can't be. He's not supposed to be back until next week,' she said to herself. But the slim, vague figure and the slanted hat were unmistakable.

'Hal!' she called, and ran toward him. The young man paid no attention to her. 'Hal.' Of course it was he. She thought so until she stepped in front of him and looked tenderly into the eyes of a perfect stranger. 'Oh, excuse me!' she said. 'I thought you . . .'

'. . . were someone else.' The young man nodded pleasantly. He was shorter and heavier than Hal, and his features were quite different. Yet in his general appearance he had been Hal's double. Even his voice was the same, as was his courteous and faraway manner.

'It's love,' Gladys said, 'when you start mistaking other fellows for him.'

'Have you had that with Johnny?'

Gladys gave a short laugh. 'Who looks like that big ape?'

She had been depressed since spending the week with Heffernan at the sawmill. Her exuberance was fitful. She accepted few dates, mostly occasional suppers with Jack Swan, the public-relations man, who didn't count. Lately she had been bringing home stacks of women's magazines. During much of her free time she lay around the apartment reading the love stories and scoring herself on such quizzes as 'Are You a Good Marriage Risk?' Twice for no reason at all she had decided not to go to work. In bed, she ate prodigious quantities of apples and stared out the window.

Rose felt sure that things must have gone wrong in Maine. When she asked about it, Gladys only murmured something insulting about the football-player.

23

Plans for September and Business Love-Making

In Arcadia Life's reception room, Jack Swan threw his cigarette away. He was more nervous than usual before going in to see Purdy. Today he was supposed to deliver his memo on publicity for the convention in September. It wasn't ready, and he knew why.

Gladys was responsible. 'From now on I'll stop kidding myself,' he swore with bitter resolve. His futile obsession with this big blonde was going to ruin him. At the office the younger fellows who worked for him were beginning to wonder. He showed up late for conferences. He didn't finish memos. When he was caught in the wrong, he tried to yell his way out of it. There was no way to explain his miserable situation to anyone.

If he could make people understand that he wasn't slipping, but sick, sick with her. She was in his dreams, but that was nothing. Her big white breasts and shoulders pushed into his mind during conferences. They interrupted his creative flow and scattered his memos. They even hampered his attempts to fulfill his weekly obligation to his wife. And all this time he wasn't getting any satisfaction from her. The one time she jumped him, he ran. 'I'm sick,' he groaned, cursing his unmanageable sexuality.

Now he had to fake some excuse to keep Purdy off his neck a little while longer. The agency-director was looking at a copy of *The Arcadian*, the company magazine that came out twice a month. 'Our friend Hingham is back. He was just here,' he said.

'Fine! When can I talk to him?' Swan had been interested in The Hingham Story since the day he heard about it. He hadn't immediately connected the name with that of the dud who went around with Gladys's roommate. When it did turn out this way, he wasn't surprised. Fate apparently intended him to hang around that apartment. He saw a story in Hingham's metamorphosis, and was eager to get at it.

'You can talk to him if you want to, but our prodigy is in pretty bad shape,' said Purdy. 'He's white and thin. His eyes are big and hollow – '

'No wonder, after what he did in Bradford.'

'He's more than tired. He looks – I can't explain it. For instance, he almost passed out when I showed him this.'

It was a cartoon in *The Arcadian*. The drawing, spread over two pages, depicted the company's leading salesmen in the garb of track stars – runners entering the home stretch. In the third position was Hal Hingham, but his figure was treated differently from the others. The artist had placed clouds of dust under his heels, and he alone was shadowed. An arrow indicated him as the Dark Horse.

'Hingham was upset, you say?'

'He acted like a road-company Hamlet. He took me by the wrist, and sort of held on to me, and shook his head, and gave me these pitiful sighs – '

'Fred!' interrupted Swan. Like that, his troubles were over. He *had* the idea he was supposed to bring into Purdy's office. 'Let me tell you – if he's handled right, Hingham can be the feature, or at least one of the features, of our convention publicity.'

He commenced speaking in the friendly but authoritative tone of the public-relations scientist explaining his world to a stranger.

'Most people are getting pretty blasé about publicity. If you really want to get noticed, the stereotyped institutional approach won't do any more. Of course, I'll get the space for the convention. We'll put out the usual institutional stuff, but this year let's go beyond that. *Personalize* the company,' Swan said, 'and here's where Hingham comes in.'

'But you heard me say, Hingham is – '

'Just hear me through, Fred. Let's build the convention around that great American legend, the Success Story. Hingham in his peculiar way is a modern Horatio Alger. Now, since the Alger concept is outmoded, we'll work in a psychiatric interpretation, like Freud. Remember Hingham's stern, old-fashioned father. Like father, unlike son. It's new!

'The obstacle facing the modern Horatio Alger is not the cold, cruel world, but the cold, cruel father. He wins this battle by freeing himself from his father's domination, which has prevented him from becoming a success. We'll get a psychiatrist to say –

individual enterprise triumphs over neurosis. It's a perfect Prodigal Son situation.'

'Wait a minute,' said Purdy. 'I enjoy your impudence, but it has nothing to do with the Prodigal Son.'

'Yes, it has,' Swan contradicted him surely. He had never felt so strong in Fred Purdy's presence. 'Hingham transferred his father image to you, and came back to you – or, better! The company takes over the father role. Hingham returns home with the fatted calf, and he's forgiven and celebrated for that amazing selling job at Bradford.'

'You certainly know how to corrupt the Bible.'

'What does it matter!' cried Swan in delight at his own ingenuity. 'The point is, I've got something.'

Fred Purdy shook his head. 'What I don't understand, Swan – you've probably never read the Bible, or Freud, or Horatio Alger, but still you have the effrontery to combine them – and it's not a bad idea.'

Swan kept his eye on the ball. 'Do you approve, Fred? I'll bang out a memo right now. You can send it to the home office tonight.'

'You realize, don't you, that Hingham isn't the top man yet? Maybe he won't be.'

'That's all right. We can always juggle the statistics. He's probably sold more over a shorter period – that's it. Create a special citation. Hingham sold more in less time – '

'Write your memo, Swan. You can do it in the conference room,' the client said. 'Remember, though, this boy is highly nervous. If you make him a center of attraction, with interviews and all that, he'll need careful handling.'

'There isn't a man who can't be handled,' said Swan grandly.

'Suppose we make Hingham your personal responsibility.'

'Fine with me,' answered Swan, as he went into the conference room. He was lighthearted again, and full of confidence.

'The New York office is on my tail about this, you realize,' Purdy said from the door.

Looking up from his typewriter, Swan felt so good that he couldn't resist putting a small needle into the client. 'What's the matter, Fred? You're secure. The securest man I know.'

He envied the way Purdy could smile and let it pass, because it was true.

* * *

Fred Purdy left the elevator boy laughing, but it wasn't until he stepped out into the street that he realized he was the butt of his own joke. Somebody beat him to a cab. He signaled to another, and missed it. He stood on the corner, inhaling the heat and fumes of the street. It was an effort to breathe. He felt a sweet sickness in the atmosphere. Normally he would have laughed over it. Today an incident had disturbed him, and he was hard put to rejoice in the corruption of the very air.

'Let's talk over your proposition at breakfast,' George Escrow had said. 'That's the best time for me.'

Breakfast! He told this to the elevator boy, partly in return for a special service – the Purdy Express from the eighth floor. The elevator dropped with amazing slowness. Through the open grill-work he watched the great coil of cables advancing up the shaft. 'I tell you,' he said to his already grinning listener, 'next thing you know people will be doing business while they make love.'

Breakfast! He recovered himself with savage good humor to ask: why not? It was perfectly logical. He had long ago become used to transacting business at lunch. He found it only mildly insane to be eating, smoking, drinking a martini, and talking in one simultaneous operation. The irony of this was worn, and not worth mentioning. And how about the club luncheons, and company banquets, and smokers? He had not revolted against them.

He had built his view of life on these splendid perversions. Without them his malice would collapse, and so would he. The good life was one sale after another. The man who let his mind wander ran the risk of glimpsing the enormous meaninglessness of his career. How often he counseled the younger salesmen to 'get lost, drown yourselves' in *it*. Although he mocked their innocent faces, he wasn't entirely kidding. It was their only hope, really, to believe that salesmanship was all of life – because then it would become so.

Why then did the idea of having breakfast tomorrow with George Escrow disturb him? The business breakfast would be only one more perversion. His objection, he supposed, came from a feeling of lost dignity – of being goosed around by commerce, and becoming simply an agent in place of a person. He remembered imagining that he belonged to his desk like a cowboy to his horse, 'like you belong to this elevator,' he added to the momentarily sobered boy.

You had to rest from continually laughing in self-defense. How? He could get drunk, but not alone, and somehow all his drunks turned into business drunks. 'There's no privacy any more,' he complained to the elevator boy. He thought of his business golf games, the poker and bridge games, the outings, picnics, and holiday get-togethers of company personnel. He hammered on it gleefully. Business Thanksgivings and Christmases, business carols and benedictions. People selling presents around the Christmas tree. Business worship!

'Yes,' he repeated to the boy, 'the next thing will be business love-making.'

'I always prefer to deal with an established firm,' Fred Purdy declared tenderly.

The real-estate woman smiled coldly at this tribute, but he knew what he was doing.

'Now that your divorce has come through,' he pointed out, 'you need protection more than ever.'

This approach immediately brought them closer together. Now he understood why she had stalled him before. His pitch had been too ardent. Where business and pleasure met, there was no room for sentiment. She bought him, and would eventually buy the policy if he didn't overplay his hand. She had weaknesses, things she liked. He touched a soft spot, jokingly: 'You're uncovered in so many unsuspected places. Let me show you.'

'Yes,' she murmured impatiently. 'Go on! Go on!'

He made his moves, and spoke of love and its obligations – to take care of dear ones.

'Oh, hurry up! Come on, convince me!' she cried, and flung out her cold, soft arms in a derisive gesture. He knew her now. It was just a matter of pinning her down. He braced himself, to get a purchase.

'Okay – ' he grinned – 'let's get down to cases.'

If marble could suddenly become soft and malleable, this was the way she yielded to him. He didn't repeat his mistake of becoming serious. There was a terrible coldness about her that no sympathy could dissipate, but, cold to cold as they were, they struck a spark, and it seemed to leap into her eyes. Flinty, passionate glances excited him beyond any measure he had counted on.

'I'm playing the game! I'm taking it all the way!' he exulted. He was going to violate everything with this beady-eyed woman. He felt all the gods in heaven looking down on him in horror. Hanging on desperately, he gripped the disordered sheets.

'What's that?' she demanded, seizing one of them, and pointing to the italicized clause at the bottom.

'The indemnity – provision.' With an efort, he showed her the explanatory paragraph in the booklet. They went on browsing through the pages together.

And now she began to pick up on the whole deal, and her comprehension came faster and faster. He had the answers before she could bring the questions to bear on him, and then he advanced again, always stronger. Her scornful eyes told him to close out the proposition, and he did, and he did. If this was hell, he felt no pain. If this was hell, it was the best hell. Their hands clapsed, and they cried out simultaneously: 'It's a deal!'

24

Deserted by Dr Modesto

The desk clerk at the Circle Hotel smiled and said there was no mail for him.

'Are you sure – nothing? No telegram or phone call from Broad View, Nebraska?' Hal asked.

'No, sir.'

The news stunned him. He couldn't believe that Dr Modesto would leave him alone in the world. He went up to his room and sat down on the bed without bothering to unpack. Was there no forgiveness for the Centralist who made one mistake? He wondered what happened to a fallen Centralist. Did he fly off into the void, unblessed, unloved because he couldn't get through to people?

He telephoned Rose, and it was the same.

'Hal, it's been so long.'

'Yes, it sure has.'

There followed silences that they kept breaking with desolutory exclamations of happiness. It was an exchange of dead love, for she was as much a stranger to him as the hotel clerk. Yet tonight he was to tell her again that he wanted to marry her.

Worst of all was the moment at Arcadia Life when Fred Purdy shook hands with him and opened up the magazine to his picture. He gazed in absolute horror at the cartoon of him in track shorts. He felt like a criminal who has seen his picture in the post office. Here was the evidence of his crime in Bradford for thousands of readers to see. Someone would surely report it to Dr Modesto. Perhaps he already knew. Hal held on to Fred Purdy's hand and tried to explain that he was in trouble and must go into hiding. He succeeded only in stammering and being agreeable.

'Mr Purdy, please – it's great . . .'

The conformist struggled to express his lost self, but he had forgotten how.

'If you don't mind, sir, I'd like to – thank you . . .'

All he could do was shake hands in agonized cheerfulness. He went out, feeling his way down the walls of the corridor. He had a sudden longing to be with Merko. Merko might teach him how to be himself again.

He grasped at the chance that Dr Modesto had not seen his letter. An assistant might have kept it from him. He bought a strip of post cards, scribbled 'Forgive Me' and 'Help Me' on the back of Paul Revere and the Tea Party, and mailed them from different post boxes to Broad View, Nebraska.

25

The Love-Date (2)

Rose couldn't stand the waiting. One moment she came to rest on the arm of the couch, and the next she was at the window. He wasn't due until eight, but might be early. In fact, she had the right to expect this from him. She leaned out the window, searching only for a figure that would be *running* toward the rendezvous. There was no such person in sight. She waited, braced against the sill until her arms ached, and then went back to the couch.

On the radio, an instrumental called 'Musical Chairs' was followed by 'The Night shall be Filled with Love.' 'If you need ready cash, here is all you have to do,' the announcer said. With six minutes to go, she turned it off and ran around fixing flowers.

The doorbell rang thirty seconds early. She hung on the door while he climbed the stairs. She dared look, and there he was in his slanted hat with the feather in the brim, offering her the long white box.

'Hal!'

'Hi there!'

She rushed to kiss him and his arms fell softly around her shoulders.

'Oh, I've missed you so much!'

'Me too.' He laughed tenderly. 'Get your coat on. We're going to Childs' Old France.'

They were orchids like the last time. He studied her with a pleased air. She noticed how thin he was from working so hard. His eyes were huge and mild, and he was much too pale. But she would fatten him up, and get him out in the sun. His hands shook when he helped her on with her coat. She regarded him coquettishly over her shoulder, and saw that he was dazed with happiness.

In the taxi he told the driver: 'Childs' Old France, and make it snappy.'

Thank God, it was the same. He hadn't changed. She cuddled

him. Suddenly she was kissed hard on the mouth. She drew away in mock fear of his uncontrolled passion. The taxi swerved, and he called out to the driver: 'Look out! I've got a valuable piece of property here. The girl I'm going to marry.'

'You gettin' married, eh?'

'Yes,' he said, 'so watch out, watch out. This is my girl.'

Something in Hal's words troubled her. Perhaps it was the way he spoke – in a faraway sing-song. They crossed the railroad bridge at Huntington Avenue. An engine passed beneath them and sent a volley of steam into the night. His fine profile moved against the cloud. He turned to her. His smiles came and went as if they were produced by wind currents.

'You don't know how I love you,' he said, and kissed her.

Her hands felt cold in her lap. She thought: 'I mustn't dream this.'

At Childs' he made a charming fuss with the waiters, and insisted on the same table. He arranged everything in a loud, smooth manner, but now she openly stared at him, unable to believe what she knew.

'Hal . . .'

He didn't notice. He was waiting, she understood, for her to go to the ladies' room, like the last time. As she moved among the tables, the band started to play. She powdered her nose in a dream in which she saw her dim drowned image wavering in the glass. She was looking down into the bottom of a pool that turned into a very dry martini.

'Have another.'

'I can't. I'll get dizzy.'

'I wish we could go on this same date forever, Rose.'

The lobster came, but she couldn't eat. She could only laugh, and reach for him and kiss him across the table, as she had done the last time.

'You don't know, Rose, you just don't know.'

Now, she realized, he was going to request the rumba.

She got up dazedly. 'Hal, please . . .'

There was a terrible sickness in his happy face.

'May I have the honor, mademoiselle?'

She had to stop him, bring him back to life, but he swept her away into the identical dance. He whispered in her ear: 'Every Friday, it will be like this.' She would have collapsed. He held her in the gentle arms of a cavalier, and said: 'We'll get out of here. All you need is a little fresh air.'

He walked her to the corner and back, and she felt much better. She took courage and vowed: 'I'll save him,' although she couldn't think of any way to do it.

'I know a swell place.' He grinned. 'The Sphinx Club. I have a certain question to ask you there.'

'No, Hal.'

He seemed not to hear, but repeated: 'A swell place.'

'Hal, darling. Listen, darling. I don't want to go to the Sphinx. We mustn't go, because you're sick. I want you to go home and rest, and then – '

'Sick?' he scoffed, good-naturedly. 'I feel fine. When we get to the Sphinx, I want to ask somebody a certain question.'

They stood under the sidewalk awning, swept by the headlights of cars turning the corner. Then Rose hit on it. She remembered the time when Gladys offered to get her a psychiatrist. 'Hal, if a doctor tells you you're sick will you believe him?'

He shook his head. 'I don't see what's wrong. Why can't it be like this forever?' he asked in bewilderment.

'It can be, dear. But it wouldn't be fair to either of us to get married when you're a little bit sick like this. You see, you've worked so hard. You're nervously upset, but the psychiatrist will know exactly what to do. And after you've rested, we can go ahead.'

'I love you also, Rose. Let's go to your place,' he said feebly.

'You see, dear? The way you're talking now – that's all part of it.'

In the end he allowed her to take him in a cab to the Circle Hotel. She kissed him. 'Now, you get a good sleep,' she said. 'I'll phone you tomorrow about the doctor.'

Seeing him walk meekly toward the hotel, she felt sad and guilty for treating him in this way. She might at least have asked him to come home with her. The taxi had passed several blocks before she decided to go back after him.

'Never mind. It's easier to walk,' she told the driver.

She hurried to the Circle Hotel, but found at the desk that he had not yet come in. 'Where is he? Walking the streets!' she thought in distress. Then she caught sight of him down the block, strolling along with his hands in his pockets.

'Hal!' He went on his way. Catching up with him, she put her hand on his elbow, and cried out in dismay as a strange young man turned and greeted her. 'Oh – you,' she exclaimed, although it wasn't the young man she had mistaken for Hal before, but another one. He too, she saw on closer inspection, bore no real resemblance to Hal, except in his vague, faraway manner.

'Excuse me.'

'Not at all.' He smiled, and tipped his slanted hat.

Hal didn't want to go to bed, and decided to take a walk on the Common. It was better in the dark. Couples were still pacing languidly along the paths. He heard a steady murmur of voices among the trees. The pinwheel by the fountain was a policeman's billy. On all sides of this peaceful haunt were the twinkling lights of office buildings and hotels. No one could find him here. If they took too much notice of him, he could come here. He wandered around the frog pond, and remained bemused for a while by a pale curl of water dipping, it seemed, motionless and silent, into the pool. The voices drifted away. The lights in the office buildings went out, window by window.

Rose said he was sick. She was going to get a doctor for him. 'Perhaps I am sick,' he thought, 'but I need someone better than any doctor.' Of course, and he had someone, the only one – Merko, who was like nobody else. Merko would understand, and tell him what to do.

A great neon clock in the sky told him that he had time to catch the milk train to Riverton. He set out for the South Station. He felt more and more alive and like a person with every step he took toward his tough little friend.

26
Joan and Merko

The milk train arrived in Riverton shortly after sunrise. Hal had a cup of coffee at the station, and walked slowly across town toward the road that led to Merko's hill. The morning air was cool and fresh. The new day and the prospect of seeing Merko made him feel cheerful and clear-headed. Perhaps, he thought, Merko might invite him to share the hilltop, and he wouldn't have to deal with the world any more.

He passed by the grounds of the Olympic Club. The early-morning sun gave the greensward an amber tint. The line of poplars at the end of the field was bathed in yellow. He glimpsed something like the flutter of a handkerchief or a small kite by the high-jumping pit. He saw that it was an athlete working out, a girl, Joan Vigoro.

He shouted and waved to her. As he approached, she turned her back on him. She ran, leaped, and went up and over the crossbar, but she brushed it with her knee and it went rattling to earth.

'Do you always work out at this time of the morning?' he asked.

'Oh, it's you,' she said, in an unfriendly tone. 'If you must know, this is my last day here.'

She stood before him in white shorts and a black jersey. Her long legs were unexpectedly full in the thighs. She was a deep-breasted girl, and her figure seemed heavier and more settled than before. He was not surprised when she said despondently, more to herself than to him: 'It's a good thing I'm quitting. I can't even get over five feet any more.'

'Where are you going, Joan?'

'To Rockton, to my husband-to-be. Would you like to know who he is? Mr Homer Schmitt, the ugliest old man I could find in the mail-order catalogue. He's a kennel-keeper. He lives in Rockton. Would you like to see his picture?' She found the photograph in her purse. 'I meet his requirements!' she laughed shrilly, handing it to Hal.

Homer Schmitt was a crafty, snaggle-toothed man of at least fifty-five. He leered out of the picture in a knowing manner.

'He wants a strong girl to fetch and carry for him. A girl "without airs," he says. I sent him a picture of myself carrying a pipe and slippers!'

'Why did you do it?' asked Hal. 'Did you have to go so – '

'What difference does it make?' she demanded bitterly, throwing her coat over her shoulders. Since no man in Riverton would have her, she deliberately offered herself at random. Now she would don her smock and take the vows of drudgery. She would rejoice as the elasticity went out of her muscles.

'That's what you expect of women,' she declared, continuing with tearful sarcasm. 'We should follow the man with a broom and dustpan in our hands. That's our job.' Very well then, no more leaping. No more vying with the boys in sawdust pits. As quickly as she could, she would become old, until her body and mind were bowed and thickened by the accumulated weight of trivial duties. And one day all the people of the town would be able to say, without a dissenter: 'There goes Mrs Homer Schmitt, a good woman.'

'What happened with you and Merko? I'm going to see him now,' Hal said.

Joan sat down on the grass and began to cry. 'Why did he have to come along? And hang around, and make me think . . .? Of course, I knew he didn't like me. He was always scowling and looking away. He'd look at me and spit on the grass – '

'That means he likes you,' Hal explained.

Joan shook her head. 'Then he'd walk away and talk with the fellows. They all do it. They watch me for a minute, and then make some excuse . . . But what I hoped was, the way he kept staring – '

'You should have given him more of a chance.'

'I did everything! Even yesterday,' Joan said. 'I put my hand on his arm, and he jumped away as if I had a disease. Some of them were watching. They laughed at the way he reacted to me. What do you care?' She turned on Hal, and he felt her resentment of him because he was a man.

'I'm going to see him now, and – '

'Leave me alone.' Joan eyed him with anger, and Hal felt that he was representing all mankind. 'You're all repulsive in your different ways. Well in exactly one hour I'm leaving this town, and sports, and this miserable club. Tonight I'll be in Rockton – engaged to the worst one of you I could find in the catalogue, and that should satisfy everybody!'

She picked up her sweater and walked away from him.

Hal trudged along the road to Merko's hill. His only trips to and from there had been by motorcycle, and he had forgotten how far it was out of town. By noon he had walked several miles. He decided to sit down and rest. There was no hurry. It would be just as well to give Joan a head start before telling Merko where she was going. He needed Merko to help him, at least for a while. There would be no place for a woman on the hilltop.

Hal dozed off. When he awoke it was already two o'clock. The hill, it turned out, was only a few hundred yards farther on. He climbed it wearily, and found Merko on his hilltop of rocks, sitting on the cottage doorstep with his chin in his hands. Hearing footsteps, Merko stood up and craned his neck. He seemed disappointed to discover that it was Hal.

'Aren't you in the mood to see me?' Hal asked.

'I'm all right. Come in,' said his friend, without enthusiasm. They went inside, and Merko brought out two bottles of beer, glasses, and large cork mats. 'Mind you don't spill it. I've just polished the table,' he said.

Hal was surprised by the change in Merko's room. A pathetic attempt had been made to create an atmosphere of complacent bourgeois comfort. Signs of disorder had virtually disappeared. Instead, Merko had arranged an interior of heavy stuffed chairs, with doilies and tablecloths everywhere, vases packed with flowers, bowls full of tropical fish, and pictures of children and flowers. He directed Hal to one chair away from the rugs, and placed a seashell ash try beside him.

Hal decided to go directly to the point. He pulled his chair close to the little man, and said: 'Merko, I've come for help. Teach me how to be myself, the way you are.'

Merko stared at the floor and didn't reply.

'Can't you help me?' Hal asked timidly.

'And I,' said Merko, 'want to be more like other people.'

They looked at one another without speaking. After a while they picked up their beers and went out among the rocks, which were already throwing long shadows down the hillside.

'I saw Joan this morning,' Hal began.

Merko groaned and swore a huge oath against women and their fickle minds. 'Of course, I don't care at all what she does. But she's a clean girl and – I want to see her get the best,' he said in a loud, careless tone.

Hal told him about Homer Schmitt. Merko walked in circles, grinding his teeth. 'That's the way they are!' he said. 'Crush your pride every time! After I offer myself, she runs off to an old fleabag – '

'Offered yourself?'

'Certainly I did.' Merko kicked at a boulder. 'I gave her every chance to understand how I felt about her. I came out with direct hints.'

Hal explained that Joan was completely unaware of any hints.

'What do these crazy women want?' Merko demanded, looking at Hal in amazement. 'What's a man supposed to tell them?'

'What did you tell her?'

'Well,' said Merko, walking with his hands clasped behind him, 'I didn't get soft. That's not my style. I said – more in actions than in words. Letting her know by using certain looks. You know. You *look* at somebody.' Merko glared at Hal. 'If they're on the ball, they intercept it.'

'You didn't say anything to her?'

'Yes, I did. Mostly under my breath, but she could have caught on if she were making the effort to listen. I said: "You've got good long muscles there, and a good style going over the bar."'

'You said that?'

'Yes, and I told her: "I'd like to practice with you sometime." She said: "What?" and I told her: "You heard me," and gave her a *look*.' Merko scowled at the clouds. 'She's gone away,' he muttered. 'It's just as well. I couldn't have gone through with it anyway. I told you women weren't my style. She'd wreck me, like they all do. It gets into your flesh. You get soft. Oh, she wasn't that way. Her flesh was clean.

'But just the same I could see it in her. She'd sink into a biological condition like all the rest of them do when they get you married. Maybe you think I'm a hermit, but I've been around, and I know marriage doesn't go with normal companionship. You have to . . . What's *that* got to do with real love? I loved her because she was too pure to touch.'

Merko's face writhed. 'Will that – old – lay his hands on her?'

'If they're married, I should think he would,' Hal said.

'And she'd let him?'

'Well, if they're married . . .'

'Impure!' Merko threw a shower of rocks into the valley.

'Wait!' Hal said, caught up in Merko's destiny. 'Maybe she wouldn't want to, but she'd be forced to.'

Merko snorted. 'She'd be strong enough to stop him if she really – '

'No, I mean forced by circumstances.'

Merko brooded on this, then put his arms out to Hal. 'Go and see her. Tell her I'd throw myself at her feet – if she asked me. Walk up Niagara Falls against the water, keep driving after her anywhere, if she was trapped. There's a mesa in the Grand Canyon, you tell her, and nobody's ever been able to get to the top of it. I would, if she was there. Anything.'

'But why don't you just tell her you love her?'

Merko's brow knotted in wrath and perplexity. He hammered the wall of his house.

'She's on the bus now. Going to him,' Hal said.

'He'll put his hands on her!'

Hal nodded.

'Let's go!' Merko rushed out. He returned to grab a vase full of roses, and ran out again. He dragged Hal down the hill to the motorcycle, and they roared off for Rockton.

Hal rode in the sidecar and hung on while Merko gunned his black charger through the dark-gold waning afternoon across landscapes of southern New England. Apple orchards, stone walls, and fields of waving corn fled past them. Dappled cows and dairy farms, red barns, rustic baseball games, billboards, gasoline stations, speed-limit signs, Lions and Rotary Club signs, End of Restricted Zones, and more corn fields rushed toward them and vanished in a roar of wind, as they plunged on. It grew darker. The clouds flattened in the west and darkened.

In the darkness ahead Hal saw the end of his life, when Merko would leave him. Glancing at his companion, who now wanted to abandon his hermitage and be like other people, he thought: 'I could stop him.' Yet he would not. On the contrary, he would help his friend escape from his own dark and empty future. He could no longer see Merko's face, but felt in the fitful gunning and maneuvering of the motorcycle the little man's fear of his first engagement with a woman. A succession of motels flashed by. Then came the flooded pennants of Rockton's used-car lots, and they rolled into the city.

27
Merko Makes It

They parked the motorcycle down the block and sneaked up on the kennel-keeper's place. The dogs began barking. Hal shrank from panting sounds near him in the dark, until he realized that they were coming from Merko. They crept past warm plants, in a summer jungle. Merko glanced apprehensively at the great overripe moon that seemed about to fall on the chimney of Homer Schmitt's house. He plucked at Hal's arm, and whispered: 'What if – ?'

'What?'

'Shhh!' Merko writhed. He was walking on tiptoe although they were still some distance from the house. 'What if they're already – ?'

'The lights are on downstairs,' Hal pointed out.

With each step forward, the expression on Merko's moonlit face became wilder and more terrified. He still held his vase full of flowers, but gingerly, as though he might at any moment throw them down and run. They sneaked closer, trying to find an open window, but all the windows were shut against the summer night. Finally Hal drew Merko to a bright pane, and they peered into the living-room.

Homer Schmitt was lording it in a big leather chair, with his slipper-shod feet on a stool, cleaning an old musket. Beside him, a frowsy hound yawned at a pile of dirty laundry in the center of the room.

'He's going to shoot her!'

'No, not with that muzzle!' Hal whispered. 'It's just an antique.'

Merko gasped. Joan had just entered the room. Her hair was tied up in ridiculously short pigtails. She stood before her husband-to-be in a painfully demure attitude, with her feet wide apart, eyes shyly lowered and her hands, already reddened from what must have been scalding dishwater, clasped in the sodden folds of her apron. After a while the old man put down the gun and beckoned to her, pointing to the hassock beside his chair. The dog bristled and made room grudgingly. Joan sat down. Homer Schmitt stroked her hair, meanwhile eating an apple and reading a newspaper.

Merko had begun a rhythmic groaning. Hal steadied him, whispering: 'It's all right! It's all right!' He was full of love for Merko in his distress. Merko's agony was beautiful. Suffering became him so. It was what he was born to do. Without malice, Hal longed for his comrade-antagonist to suffer eternally. But then, the next moment, he felt a terrible decency rising through these thoughts, saying: 'He is your brother, help him,' and he demurred: 'No, and lose him forever,' and the voice repeated: 'Help him,' and he turned toward this incredible little man who had made his life worth living a while longer.

He saw a coward. Merko fell groaning away from the window.

The old man yanked playfully at Joan's pigtails. Repeating the act several times seemed to inspire him. With ungainly elation, he leaped across the room and threw the covers off a piano. He turned a knob and the instrument began twanging 'Yes, Sir, She's My Baby.' He snapped his fingers and made her cavort with him. Hal was about to shut his eyes, when the old man tired.

The old man stood back, signaling for Joan to dance alone. Now Hal could not watch. He saw Merko cringing in the bushes and suddenly, against his own interests, beckoned fiercely for him to get up and be a man.

'I'm not yellow,' Merko said, as if reciting this fact to himself. *'I'm not yellow!'*

'What is it?'

'If she wouldn't expect me to touch her.'

'But look what's happening to her now,' Hal urged.

Homer Schmitt was back in his chair, dozing, and Joan still danced by herself. Her arms fell in a limp V. Her hands joined in the soggy apron. She seemed to have no idea where she was. The dog barked. The old man stirred and woke to his dancing bride-by-mail. He leered at her and made excited motions, pointing to the door. Joan went out, and he rushed after her.

'I think they're going upstairs,' Hal reported. He heard a crackling in the bushes, and Merko was standing beside him.

But Homer Schmitt returned, clad in pajamas. He turned off the piano. He went back to his chair and posed himself in his absurd and vulgar pantomime of lordliness, waiting for the girl to come to him. The dog pricked up his ears. Joan appeared in the doorway. She was dressed as before, except that her apron was off, her sleeves rolled up, and her blouse open at the throat. The old man made an imperious gesture, and she stepped forward, offering him a dish of pie, knife, and fork.

Schmitt seized them and began eating. Joan retired into some shadows, watching him. He took several rapid mouthfuls, and then stopped chewing. He gazed at her in anger and disbelief. From the shadows she seemed to beg him: 'What's wrong?' Still looking at her, he handed the pie dish to the dog.

Merko was taking his coat off. Homer Schmitt resumed munching on his apple core. The dog regurgitated the pie. Dog and man looked at the weary girl in the doorway. The animal gave a short bark. Schmitt nodded at Joan and jerked his thumb toward the dirty laundry. Then the night was filled with flying glass.

Through the shattered pane Hal watched Merko rush, not at Homer Schmitt, but past him, to the musket lying across the table. Schmitt gave a cracked yell and tottered up from his chair. While Joan cowered against the wall, Merko broke the old man's musket across his knees. He simply tore it to pieces. He tore the trigger out of it. Ignoring the dog, which had fastened on to his trouser leg, he went on and on making kindling of the ancient firing-piece. The old man cried frantically: 'Sic 'em! Sic 'em!' to his impotent dog, but the creature was sent flying by a thrust of Merko's leg.

Then Merko stood before Joan Vigoro and shouted in a mighty voice: 'I love you!'

She held out her arms to him, but he backed away, pointing his fist at Homer Schmitt. 'I won't have anything to do with an insulted woman. Hit him!'

'Oh, never mind that. I love you, Merko, I love you.'

'Prove it!' he demanded, shooting his fist in the direction of the terrified Schmitt.

'I'll sue your whole outfit!' the old man bawled. Scrambling to escape, he tripped and collapsed in the mound of his own foul sheets.

'Hit him!' Merko demanded once more, but without much conviction, for the enemy of his bride's honor appeared to be unconscious, and even his dog had scuttled away with terror-stricken yaps to some remote room upstairs.

And now, Hal saw, the Human Fly had come to the end of the

line. It was time for Merko to confront his lifelong nightmare, put up or shut up, make it or not. A woman's clinging arms were reaching for him. The flesh of her lips threatened him with the feast he could not but must stomach for the sake of love.

Hal lurked at the window, aware suddenly of the scent of Merko's roses and the chill feel of the vase in his hands. Waiting to see what would happen to his brother, and therefore to him, he heard clocks. They were chiming up and down the street. Altogether, it was fifty-six o'clock.

He looked inside and saw his friend retreat from the loving girl. Merko's arms were at his sides and he seemed, like an exhausted boxer gazing upward at the clock, to be searching the walls for a way out of the punishment that was coming to him. And the girl moved after him, repeating: 'Merko, I love you!' in a soft voice. At their feet the old man from the sanctuary of his dirty laundry gazed pop-eyed at this spectacle. Merko was moving toward the window, perhaps hoping to backdive out, when Hal leaned in and whispered: 'Yellow belly!'

Merko screwed his eyes shut. His features dilated in agony; he went in for the kiss, and made it.

Hal turned away from the window. He felt his life's energy draining out of him. 'It's great to see young people in love,' he thought perfunctorily. But this was no young person. It was Merko, the rock, the only one who was not part of everybody else, whom he had counted on always to remain his opposite and end his days in incorruptible misery. Gone . . .

The door opened. Merko crossed the threshold, carrying Joan and staggering ('How weak he is already,' Hal thought) into the moonlight. Hal walked toward them. He couldn't think of anything to do but hold out the vase of roses. Merko shook his head and gasped over his shoulder: 'Be back in a minute!'

Hal stood in a gravel driveway watching him bear Joan off down the deep hill. They went beyond the kennels – away from the growling, baying dogs whose shapes he made out leaping behind wire fences. Merko carried her across a dry brook and then into a field of black, waving grass.

Hal sat down and smoked a cigarette. He didn't mind waiting. Merko had said he would be coming right back. He would wait for his friend, who always kept his word. Merko always made it, through swamp and flames, when he said he would. Nothing could stop him.

He noticed a whirlpool effect in the long grass, becoming gradually slower, and still. Then the night was rent by a war whoop. This too slowly died away.

Hal walked down the road, and no sound followed him but the barking of caged dogs. On the highway he hailed a bus to Boston.

The Revelations
of Dr Modesto

PART THREE

28

The Depths of August

Rose and Hal walked across the Common on their way to the psychiatrist's office. Stealing another look at his expressionless smile, she knew she was not imagining things. 'He's sick,' she told herself again. But of what? She prayed that, as Gladys promised, Dr Mortimer would know.

She held his inert hand and gaily swung his unresisting arm to fool the passers-by. She peered uneasily into the blank friendliness of her lover's face. He wasn't even annoyed at being asked to visit a psychiatrist.

'Hal, dear,' she said. 'What are you thinking?' She squeezed his fingers and after a moment received an answering pressure. 'Hal.'

He smiled at her, blinking in the sunlight.

'Hal, I hope – '

'Yes,' he said, 'I love you more than life itself. You're all I could ever want. I dream about you at night. I'm the luckiest guy in the world, and you're the swellest girl I could ever hope for. I want it to go on like this forever.'

He stopped, placing his hands under her elbows, and kissed her. He put her hand back on his. They walked on. He swung her hand a bit, and pressed it.

'I was worried, dear,' she said. 'I thought you might resent our appointment.'

'Who, me?'

'It might have seemed that I didn't trust you.'

Again that gentle smile was turned on her, and he declared: 'Well, you've got to find out about one another. Too many marriages go on the rocks because people don't get to know about one another. It's better to find out ahead of time than later. We are doing the wisest possible thing. Isn't that right?'

'Yes, it's absolutely right!' she cried, with a sudden anguish she couldn't hide from him.

He looked at her curiously. Knowing he would pat her shoulder, she turned away from him, and then his lips were quietly and firmly on hers, and off, and he was apparently gazing into her eyes.

'That's love, isn't it?' he said.

'What's love?' she cried desperately into this courteous face.

'Why,' he said, 'you know, Rose. You know what love is. A fellow can't live without you. You're crazy about him. You can't get one another out of your minds. You can't wait for that day – '

'Hal!'

She pulled away from him.

The swan boats were circling on the pond.

'And sometimes you have little quarrels,' he said with a grin.

She couldn't answer him. He ducked away, and reappeared holding out a bunch of violets.

'A flower for mademoiselle?'

She grasped the violets, staring straight ahead of her at a candid-camera man who had just snapped their picture. The man handed Hal a big orange card. He laughed: 'Hey, thanks,' and slipped it in his pocket.

'Come on, honey,' he said. 'How about a ride on the swan boats?'

They glided on the hot black water. Behind them the nice young man in the yachting-cap pedaled between the wooden swans. A fly buzzed over rows of vacant chairs. They were drifting together in blazing silence.

It was their love – safe, flat, eternal, circling in an artifical lake, in flat water incapable of wave or eddy. They bumped.

'It's the end of the ride,' he said. 'Let's do it again.'

She couldn't think why not. 'Again?' Was there any reason why not?

'Why not, honey?' he said in her ear.

'Again?' asked the nice young man.

Trinity Chimes were sounding. She roused herself.

'No, no, the doctor . . .'

'We have to go to the doctor,' he said, smiling at the boatman.

She kept her eyes fixed on Dr Mortimer's diploma. The *National Geographic* in her lap had not been opened. Instead, she prayed to the god with the mustache and horn-rimmed spectacles whom she glimpsed through the half-open door as Hal went in. She wondered if he realized how much depended on his ability to get to the bottom of Hal's mind. A love, a marriage. She trembled at the risk she was taking. The stake was so high. With her hands twisted in her skirt, she prayed that Dr Mortimer's kindly analysis would bring Hal back to life.

Her heart leaped as the door opened. She stood up. He was shaking hands with the doctor. Then Hal came toward her, grinning as she retreated. 'Be right with you, honey,' he said, and went off to the washroom.

Dr Mortimer was beckoning to her.

She shook her head.

He beckoned again, impatiently. 'Come here, please.'

He regarded her gravely. 'Miss, your fiancé is probably the best-adjusted individual I have ever talked with. He's friendly and co-operative. He likes people, and has done well on his job. He seems perfectly normal and happy, and looks forward to marriage. However, he is a very tired boy on the verge of nervous exhustion. Since I can find nothing in his emotional make-up that would cause this, I strongly suspect that he is being *driven* by someone dear to him – someone who herself may be ridden by the very anxieties she is transferring to him.'

'But,' Rose faltered, 'I know that he's – '

'My dear, we have some time. Would you mind coming in, please?'

'Doctor, isn't Hal sick?'

'No, he's just tired. I suspect that he's much better friends with the world than you are.'

'If the world thinks Hal is all right, then the world isn't normal either!' Rose burst out.

Dr Mortimer smiled. 'I've told him we were going to talk a bit,' he said. 'Hal understands.'

29

How My Life is Spent

Swan used to wonder about the direction of his life. Now there was no need to ask. It always led to the same place – down the corridor to Fred Purdy's office. He dragged his sleeve across his sweating hairline, and made a clawing gesture, fighting his way out of August. He felt desperate for a vacation. But it wasn't that, really.

He'd had a vacation once, and gone off to Black Pond and fished miserably. The humming woods filled with strange awks and cackles had frightened him. The stink of his bait made him sick. In the evening the laughter of children on the beach, while a huge flat moon shone on the water, gave him the willies. His wife had stirred in the deck chair next to his. Her blouse was wide open at the throat, and her drowsy, girlish regard unnerved him. She seemed to expect him to get up and dance in the moonlight. He found that he was smoking two cigarettes at once. There had been an awful loneliness with her. If she could have had kids to keep her busy . . . He had seized her hands. 'I've got to get back. I've got to, honey.' He beat it back to the city.

Now, three years later, she wanted to try to make their marriage warm again. 'Can't we start over, Jack?' she asked, holding out her arms to him. He avoided her arms and her eyes. He respected his wife, and knew she understood that he was sexually involved somewhere else. Considering her now, in comparison with Gladys, he despised Gladys for the stupid female ox she was. Yet the threat that the night might come when he would take part in some enormous perversion with that splendid body held him trapped. 'God, no,' he told his wife. 'I can't take a vacation now with the Arcadia Convention coming up.' He jammed on his hat and left the house.

He needed a vacation, but from life itself. He needed a new perspective. The trouble was, he couldn't afford the time. While he was re-examining his life, others would steal a march on him.

There would have to be a time-out whistle, with everyone required to fall into the same reverie . . .

Swan slept raggedly and waked up with a crushed feeling around his eyes. There was no discharge from the war. Purdy would be on top because he hadn't got the mayor lined up. He would have to sidetrack him – bear down heavily on the Hingham publicity. But first, for God's sake, he had to find Hingham and talk with him.

He heard laughter from Purdy's office. To the good. He stepped inside and paused. Someone, apparently a young salesman, was leaning across the desk and laughing in the agency-director's face. And Fred seemed not to mind.

'You're absolutely right,' the fellow said. 'A rest. That's what I need. Ha, ha. Just get lost, exactly according to your suggestion. I'll do that.'

'That's the idea,' said Purdy in a caressing tone Swan had never heard him use before. 'It's your old home town. You haven't been back for years. That Tercentenary business ought to be a lot of fun.'

'A big celebration! It will help me relax!' The salesman grasped Purdy's hand.

'Right, and in a week or so I'll get in touch with you. You'll be at your aunt's – '

The salesman turned swiftly, colliding with Swan. 'Sorry!' he cried.

'I'm glad you two have run into each other,' said Fred Purdy. 'Hal, this is Jack Swan – the fellow who's going to handle the interviews and stories about you. Jack, this is Hal.'

Swan gazed with misgivings into a countenance of wild-eyed friendliness.

'Hal,' Purdy said, 'I wonder if you'd mind waiting in the conference room while Jack and I have a word. Then I think he wants to get together with you for a few minutes in regard to publicity and all that.'

'What's he so upset about?' asked Swan, after Hingham had gone out.

'This,' said Purdy, pushing the latest copy of *The Arcadian* across his blotter. Swan looked at a boxed-in photograph of Hingham's head and shoulders. The caption read:

HE STANDS OUT FROM THE CROWD
Hal Hingham, 3rd-Place Winner,
Toppled All Summer Records

'Well, it's a natural reaction – nothing to worry about,' said Swan uneasily.

'Of course not,' his client agreed pleasantly. 'You still intend to handle him, don't you?'

'Certainly, Fred.'

'I'm glad. The home office has accepted my recommendation that we build part of our campaign around Hingham. In addition, he will speak at the convention. They note that it's a departure from company policy to emphasize the work of one man, but in this case they'll go along. Now, as regards the rest of it, how about the mayor? Have you got him?'

Swan coughed as he was about to light his cigarette, blowing out the flame. He worked his lighter.

'I'd say – ah. I've got the mayor, Fred, that's definite. Barring the fact that he may go to the Black Hills. But if he's here, he'll present Hingham with the scroll. Then he'll speak before the Convention for two minutes – in the course of which, Fred, I'm going to have him mention that he himself is an Arcadia policy-holder. It will look fine for us in the papers, don't you think? Now, about TV and radio . . .'

Swan had long ago been forced to distinguish between official truth and real truth. There was also the truth of appropriateness. It was officially true, for instance, that the mayor was an Arcadia Life policy-holder, although in fact he was not. Similarly, he had the mayor, despite the fact that Hallahan was almost surely going to be in the Black Hills. What Swan had was Mayor Hallahan's official presence at the Convention. The speech Hallahan had not written, including the remark about the policy he did not have, would be read by somebody else.

'Albrecht is definitely interested in a Hingham interview, either live or on film. The only thing is the weather. If it doesn't rain, the night game might blanket our time. One more thing – Hingham's speech. I'll – '

'Just don't let him know that he's going to speak to the Convention – not until the last moment,' Purdy said.

'Right. I'll go in and sound him out now, and report back to you in a couple of minutes.'

Swan went into the conference room, and Hingham stood up to greet him.

'Nice to have you back, Hal. That was a great record you set.' Swan sat down opposite the man who would be his property for the next few weeks. 'As Fred told you, we want to set up a little publicity on the job you did. You know, contrasting your previous – shortcomings – with the terrific breakthrough. This means articles in the paper, some interviews – '

Hingham blanched and turned away.

'Oh, now wait,' said Swan reproachfully. 'Don't worry. I handle this kind of thing all the time. I promise you there'll be nothing embarrassing. You'll see. Right now, this is just a preliminary. I want to get a line on your true personality.

Hingham raised his head and whispered: 'I haven't any.'

'That's all right,' said Swan. 'I'll create one for you. What would you rather be? Young and arrogant – humble, conscientious – modest – ?'

'Yes.'

'Fine. We'll go on the modesty basis. I'll cook up some stories, and we can get together in a week or so to work out your dialogue. Don't worry, Hal,' Swan repeated, getting up. 'By the way, haven't I met your fiancée – that nice looking girl, Rose, who rooms with Gladys?'

'Yes, she's the sweetest girl in the world.'

'I believe you. Well, okay, Hal, good to have had this talk. We'll be in touch after the end of the week.'

'It was a good idea, your sending him on vacation,' Swan said to Fred Purdy. 'Frankly, he's in no shape at all. Where's he going? You'll have to give me his address.'

'Here,' said the agency-director. 'He's from Hampton. The town is celebrating its Tercentenary. I suppose there will be some laughs for all.'

'Three hundred years old – the way I feel,' joked Swan. The fact was that he felt better than he had for some time, and was not really worried about Hingham's condition. Given the right material, he would be okay. Swan knew that no man was better or worse than his material.

'I'll keep track of him through his girl friend. The first principle is, whenever you can, operate through *la femme*,' he said jauntily. 'I'm going over there around six.'

* * *

Swan drove to the Charles Street walk-up, remembering the humiliating evenings he had spent with Gladys and her football-player. Today he felt stronger. Perhaps he was in a low period of his sexual cycle. He felt he had so much momentum worked up that he might pay practically no attention to his blonde fetish, and stick to his business with Rose.

It was Rose who opened the door. 'I've come to see you – about Hal,' Swan explained, smiling. He made a point of not asking for Gladys. He told Rose about Hal's success, and the publicity that would be arranged to honor him. She nodded happily, although, he noted, with some reserve. 'It will give him confidence,' she said.

'Not to mention some extra moolah for the honeymoon,' put in Swan. But she didn't respond.

'I know what you're thinking,' he said. 'You don't think Hal is very well, do you?'

She began to cry quietly into her handkerchief.

'Did you ever think of sending him to a psychiatrist, Rose – I mean, after the Convention?'

She sobbed. 'I did. Dr Mortimer said to leave him alone – that he was under too much pressure.'

'There you are. That's what we want to avoid, right? Because as it gets close to Convention time, he will have to be under some pressure. Our job will be to shepherd him through; so, to begin with, Mr Purdy has sent him on a week's vacation to his home town – Hampton. Here's the address; it's his aunt's house. Now, will you make sure to keep in touch with him, or the aunt, and let me know every day what he's doing? Okay? In that way, we can . . .'

Swan paused, in fascination. Through the half-open door leading to the bedroom, he saw the bathroom door move, and Gladys emerged naked, the first time he had seen her so. She passed before the mirror, and stopped to consider herself. The view of her splendid white back made him faint with desire. Then she turned, and he saw that the great body that had nearly ruined his life had undergone a change, thickened, and become softly massive and gentle. Gladys did not stride any more, but planted her feet carefully, turned slightly outward. She was not admiring, but examining her new contours. He caught a glimpse of lusterless, staring eyes. She was eating an apple.

And all at once, in this moment, he was free of her. The magnificent body he had fearfully lusted after had been returned to nature to carry on, presumably, the Irish race. Thick, soft, and quiescent, Gladys's great blond frame was obviously no longer capable of the gymnastics he had dreamed about. She was a cow, no more attractive to him than any other woman. He would as soon make a pass at Rose, he thought, with a dart of malice.

'Doll,' he said to Rose, 'you and I will see to it that Hal gets through all right. Will you remember to keep in touch with me now?'

'I'll do everything I can,' answered Rose in a dispirited tone, seeing him to the door.

'And give my regards to your roommate. Tell her I'll see her around,' he said in a loud voice.

30

On the Train

'Atlantic!' cried the conductor in the nearly empty car. 'Haven't I seen you somewheres?'

'I guess – '

'Let's see your ticket. Hampton, I thought so. You're a Hampton boy.'

'I'm a Hampton boy.'

'I knew it. Maybe you've been away, but no matter. It doesn't rub off. Going back down for the Tercentenary?'

'Yes, I am.'

'I could tell. Well, it's the biggest day Hampton will ever have, I imagine.'

'Yes,' Hal said, looking out the window. The pane was spotted with rained-on coal dust. He considered the mud flats and the tilted masts of skiffs stranded at low tide. Yellow mists moved about the bay. A boy leaped off some decaying piles into the shallows and came up holding his nose amid a spray of mud.

He felt himself in the middle of a big endless day, not at all like any day he had ever known. He turned anxiously to the conductor and said: 'It is bigger, isn't it. All stretched out. It covers the whole future.'

'Past and future,' the conductor amended. 'It covers everything the town was, and foreshadows what it hopes to be. I hated to miss the pageant, but we've been past there twice today already, and you should see the square. Everybody's walking around in their Pilgrim costumes. They've got to dress up in some kind of costume. That's the law today. And there's bands – music.'

'Rexford!'

The train paused beside what looked like a large outhouse, and no one got off or came aboard.

'North Burnham next!' The conductor went on about the celebration he wouldn't be able to witness. 'There's a lot of tradition in that town. Of course, after three hundred years you're bound to get a certain amount of it.

'North Burnham. You know, you hate to miss anything that only happens once in three hundred years, no matter what it is. Whatever stays in one place that long is worth looking at, I believe.

'Burnham!'

'Look!' Hal pointed. On the station platform he saw two forms of himself, identical young men in slanted hats, in vague attitudes, watching the trains go by.

'Couple of Hampton fellows?' inquired the conductor.

Hal fell asleep and dreamed he was dead. Death was a flat bright eternity in which people kept talking to him, not understanding that he wasn't there. Or, rather, they persisted in speaking to forms of him he had long since discarded or had not yet assumed. He tried everything to capture popular acceptance. He fought to get through to these others, and make them at least *see* him. He couldn't. He was forced to stand by helplessly and watch his spurious forms distract them.

He dreamed he pursued this multitude of fakers, and tried vainly to cram them back into his being. This irritated the people. One of them in a conductor's uniform said: 'Wake up – you're home.'

'Accept me,' he pleaded.

'Hampton!'

31

The Tercentenary Parade

He stepped off the train into the riotous square that was filled with Pilgrims and painted Indians. Bandsmen in red, white, and blue uniforms had assembled in the parking-lot across from the railroad station. A tuba, catching the sun, made a large gold flash in the late afternoon. The crowds moved through muffled, desultory drum-beats. There were firecrackers. A clown ran around with a cowbell.

A man in a black suit and black derby came at him, shouting: 'You're a clown!' This one didn't intend to brutalize him, but was anxiously appealing to his sense of civic responsibility. He held forth the splash of violent colors, the clown suit that needed to be filled, begging: 'It's the last one! Be a sport.'

All his life Hal had wanted to be a sport, and now he had finally made it. He was the biggest sport of all time.

The official seized him. He was passed from hand to hand, and thrust into a Pilgrim stockade that enclosed the men's dressing-room. He zippered on the clown suit. As the conical dunce cap was clapped on his head, a tremendous fanfare started up in the square, and there was a great shuffling of feet.

'Hurry, paint his face,' urged the nervous official in the black derby.

The make-up man squinted at Hal.

'Bob Pierce!'

'Mr Pierce. They started the parade!

'Oh, God. I told them *not* to!' moaned Bob Pierce, wringing his derby.

The make-up man suddenly put down his tools.

'Where are you going? Finish his face.'

'Nuts,' the technician said. 'I'm going to watch the parade.'

'No clown is leaving my stockade without a face on.'

The make-up man walked out.

'Oh, God,' said Bob Pierce. 'Here. Come here.' He drew Hal to him. 'There now. White – red. I'll spot you up a bit – all we can do. Hurry, turn sideways. Now your mouth. Darn it – now see what I've done. I painted your lips sideways and curved down. I've made you sullen and sad. Never mind. It won't do you any good to smile. Just kick up your heels. All right, hurry! Hurry up and catch the others. Good luck!'

He ran down Main Street alongside the unwinding parade. He didn't know where he belonged. There were other clowns, he saw, but all of them had their places with one contingent or another. And all but he had expressions of lunatic joy painted on their faces. He tried to join a formation of Odd Fellows. They laughed and swung their quarterstaffs at him.

'Hey, Pagliacci!'

'That's the saddest clown I ever saw!'

The firemen refused to let him sit on their truck. He couldn't approach the Boy Scouts. He paused amid the uproar of aimless hilarity – a lone, sullen clown sticking out of the joyous afternoon like a sore thumb. A tin lizzie full of Pilgrims and Indians rolled by, and the band wound up and let go:

'OH, THE MONKEY WRAPPED HIS TAIL AROUND THE FLAGPOLE!'

And as he loitered beside all this brutal merriment, feeling the old terrible pangs of loneliness, he suddenly realized that he was back where he started from. They didn't recognize him. They would refuse to know where he had been, or the things he had done. He would conquer every city but this one. He would always collapse here, and be the stranger with a poor mouth.

He started to run again, to make them accept him, but encountered an endless column of indifference. Boy Scouts, Sea Scouts, Girl Scouts, Brownies, Odd Fellows, Firemen, Mad Hatters, Damon Boys, Pythian Sisters, the Alakazam Social Club, Red Cross, Gray Ladies, Rotary, Lions, and Kiwanis, and the John Sprague Makepeace American Legion Post #73 Band all passed him by.

The whole framework of his contented life parted and burst away, and he felt as he had when he was ten years old – so panicky that he had become lost on Main Street, of all streets, and called out after his father, who had left him there as a test of self-reliance.

Then all the paraders started to laugh at him and poke him off. Dodging poles, bats, and muskets, he sought to identify himself with one group or another, while the spectators lining Main Street laughed to see such a sport. It was no doubt part of the game, a feature of the parade. This must be the Tercentenary Jester.

At last he discovered a place next to the band, whose members were too busy for horseplay. He found peace by the slide trombone and the bass drum, as the parade moved under the great elms of Main Street. He thought shamefully: 'If Dr Modesto could see me now.' Yet in spite of his dread at being home again, he felt some small excitement returning to his life. He asked, without knowing what he meant: 'Is it too late for me?'

A sharp whistle penetrated these thoughts. It was the kind boys make through their two fingers, of gang calling to gang, and he had no gang. He would cower over the game of checkers he was playing with himself. 'Aunt Mary!' Alone in the house with her, a glimpse of his father, and alone again. They marched by the place where the drunken man had chased him down the hill. Farther on, the boy had set off the firecracker under his dog. He had known which one it was, and had dared not do anything about it. Yet there was the sweet and incomprehensible afternoon when the same boy came swooping out of the woods and helped him home with his broken bicycle. God knew he had wanted to play with them, and be regular, but instead he played cribbage with his aunt. When the parades came down the street, he bolted for the attic. His father came along enough to force him to collect stamps. He thought of the caterpillar he had kept in a tin can that emerged one day as a shattered, enfeebled tiger swallowtail which he had thus ruined before birth.

> 'BEER, BEER FOR OLD HAMPTON HIGH —
> YOU BRING THE COCKTAILS, I'LL BRING THE RYE . . .'

They were marching by the clump of evergreens and the ole swimmin' hole he never swam in. Then he saw his aunt's house.

> 'SEND SOMEBODY OUT FOR GIN —
> DON'T LET A SOBER PERSON IN!'

176

The clown with the sullen mouth galloped down the side street, and the parade went on without him.

He knelt by the crumbling old lady, the companion of his childhood, who caressed his hair and wondered at his clown costume. Her hand was like a faded cushion on his shoulder. She smelled of balsam and clean linen kept in a closet for years. On the table beside her, the buff thimble, the tiny scissors, and the kit of dry threads formed a still life of which, until she moved, she was an integral part.

He heard the dainty little voice as if it came from one of the house's darkest corners: 'How you have grown up, Harold. You were always too shy to march in the parade.'

'What was I like, Auntie? I can't remember.'

'You were a shy little boy. I used to say you'd never grow up, like Peter Pan. Oh, how angry your father was!'

His head was aching and he felt cold. 'Aunt Mary, was he ever kind to me?'

'He was good to you, dear.'

'Good?' he said. 'I don't remember. Could he have been good *and* unkind?'

She touched him and whispered: 'Poor boy, you're in a fever. Come to the kitchen.'

Gently she washed the paint from his face. Sweating and coughing, he struggled out of the clown suit.

'You ought to go to bed, dear.'

He shivered.

'Go to sleep,' she said in his ear. 'Your room is just the way you left it.'

'But what will I do when I wake up, Auntie?'

She held up one finger and smiled mysteriously. He heard church bells. She was gone. He lay down in the dark bedroom. His head throbbed against his forearm. The idea of going to church some day comforted him. He saw a great dark church blazing with candles. The bells went on for a while. As he dozed, his fever increased. His aunt called the doctor and went to the kitchen to make hot tea and honey, to make him perspire. But his clothes were already drenched with perspiration when he got up and staggered and fell to the floor.

32
Back to Life

He woke to a strangely cool morning. From his upstairs room he looked across three back yards, and in each of them householders were raking leaves. There was the thump of foot on leather, and a swarm of helmeted little boys piled up in the meadow. He smelled leather, wood smoke, and burning leaves, and wondered where the autumn had come from.

He felt that he was tinder-dry and light enough to be carried away by any wind. His body rustled between the sheets. His hands drifted to rest on the coverlet. He was well, and purified and exhausted forever. The sickness had taken his blood and marrow, leaving him a perfect man of parchment with weak tea in his veins. He had never felt so listless and so well.

'Aunt Mary!' he called.

She came running in with an ice-bag and fitted it on him like a gray and black checkered beret. But then she chanced to look in his eyes, and saw the dull sign of life in them. 'Oh, thank God, Harold!' She pressed her webbed cheek against his. 'You poor boy. You've come back.'

'What do you mean, Auntie?' he asked. 'Where have I been?'

'Never mind,' she murmured. Her hand explored his exhausted face. 'I told them you would get well. You are well, aren't you, dear?' she inquired anxiously. 'I told them God would not send you there and leave you, because you are a good boy.'

At this he roused himself a bit, and gazed at her mournfully from under the ice-bag. 'How long have I been sick, Auntie?'

'Nearly two weeks, dear.'

She explained what had happened to him, and he remembered some of it. After the church bells, he had fallen with a sigh at Aunt Mary's feet. The doctor took his temperature and threw the thermometer away. It was a searing fever. He cried out against his father and invoked a pair of pagan gods named Modesto and

Merko to destroy the old man. They wrapped him in wet sheets. He was inflamed from head to foot. Even his toes ached. He writhed if someone touched his hair. Begging protection against two vipers called Purdy and Swan, he made continual pushing gestures, as if to ward off the whole world.

It was a life-and-death need to keep people at a distance, because every time he became intimate with them they stole part of him. He was growing smaller and smaller. Help! They packed him in ice. He sang all the verses of 'The Star Spangled Banner,' but they wouldn't let him alone. His very blood, the linings of his brain and liver, everything about him was inflamed, including his imagination. He thought a motorcycle was pursuing him.

He had visitors – the nice Mr Purdy and Mr Swan – but he got it into his head that they were pallbearers and shouted for them to disappear, until they did. Mr Swan sent flowers. He sent the doctor a quartz cigarette case with a note: 'There's more in it for you if you get him on his feet before September 20.'

'They seem very anxious about you, dear,' Aunt Mary said proudly. 'They phone from Boston every day.'

'Tell them,' he said, 'I'm going to Nebraska.'

'But first you must go to Boston.' She nodded brightly and replenished his ice-bag.

A rather plain girl named Rose had wept over him and gone away. But she came back on her vacation, and helped Aunt Mary with the dishes. She hung around. She left two tickets to a football game. They were all going to the game together when he got well; her girl friend's fiancé was playing in it. 'Do things together,' the psychiatrist had said. 'Do it yourself!' he roared at her, twisting about in the bedclothes. 'Easy, boy,' said the doctor, needling him. He threw the covers off, but they tucked him in like a baby. They were in league with the grinning mailmen who kept his letters from reaching Dr Modesto. Over and over again he had mailed his frantic calls for help, and there was no answer.

'Mr Purdy and Mr Swan asked me not to mention it until you got better, but they want to see you right away.' Aunty Mary propped up his pillows. 'It must be something very important.' She brought him his breakfast tray. The autumn sun warmed his tea and toast. He ate dazzling scrambled eggs, and the big glass of orange juice was like an alarm.

'We mustn't be lazy just because we were sick.'

The tart note in Aunt Mary's voice made him look at her in surprise. She had never spoken to him in this way. Then he saw that she was wearing a corsage of pink roses, and quartz earrings, and she said: 'Now, we've promised Mr Swan you would call him this morning.'

He had to get away. They were all in league against him, even Aunt Mary. He stole into the closet and found his clothes. He came out on wobbly legs, already faint from the effort of dressing – sloppy, unbuttoned, but still dressed – and sneaked downstairs. He heard pots and pans in the kitchen. He could make it now, stagger to the fields and hide in the grass until night, then escape to Nebraska . . .

Silently he eased the door open and slipped outside. A creaking sound made him turn. Rose was swinging in the hammock. She was waiting for him on the front porch, with two bags packed. One was his. She regarded him with a steadfast love, but at the same time she was swinging a handbag with a big quartz buckle.

33

Pressure on Jack Swan

Fred Purdy had forgotten that everything was made for laughs.

'Aside from not being able to produce Hingham, after having promised the papers you would,' he said, 'what's this I hear about the mayor?'

Swan put a trembling cigarette in his mouth. 'Fred, Hallahan went to the Black Hills after all. It was one of those things. I even called the State House, and I would have been able to get Ernie Ransom to stop him, but Ernie – '

'In other words, the mayor isn't going to be with us Monday,' the client said.

'Well, he is in a sense. City Hall approved the speech, and the acting mayor, that's Barris, will read it on Hallahan's behalf. As for Hingham, please don't give up hope yet. The aunt tells me he's coming out of it. She says he doesn't look too bad, and we've got seventy-two hours yet. If they do get him up here, I've got a terrific program – he's already fixed up for a Sunday feature in the *Herald*. He's on radio – the Helen Crabtree show, and *Young America Speaks*. On TV, we've got a spot on *Success Story*.

'Also, the speech I've written for Hingham is, if I do say so, really memorable. The papers have advance copies. He pays tribute to Arcadia, and you, Fred, and what life insurance stands – '

'Swan,' said the agency-director, 'I don't suppose it's polite to break into one of your pipe dreams, but I'm sick of your glibness, and excuses, and general inefficiency. For instance, you talk of seventy-two hours. In other words, assuming that by some miracle Hingham could be in Boston tomorrow, you expect me to believe that you would see him through all those interviews, and so forth. But I know where you'll be tomorrow – at that football game for another, and much smaller, account. Why do you kid me?

'Perhaps you don't understand me. You think I'm a caustic but easygoing chap. You're probably aware that I don't care about this

Convention nonsense, and don't believe in it. But my attitude is a luxury, you see. I can only have it so long as I'm successful. Once I slip – '

He was interrupted by the telephone. The call was for Swan, who shot out of his chair to pick up the receiver.

'Hello,' he said. 'No!' he cried in incredulous joy. 'Here *now*? Hold him, I'm coming!'

Swan reached for his hat. 'It's what's-her-name, the girl. She's with Hingham at his room in the Circle Hotel. I'm going to get you that publicity this afternoon.' At the door, he said recklessly: 'Perhaps you are sorry for some of those words, Fred.'

34

The Hal Hingham Story

Hal clutched handfuls of letters and post cards and let them fall about him like confetti. 'Dear,' Rose said, 'they're compliments for you,' and went around picking them up.

The hotel room turned quietly. His picture was on the cover of *The Arcadian* and the caption said: 'HOTTEST UNDERWRITER.' He examined with renewed astonishment the confidential interview some writer had apparently held with him. They must have had someone impersonating him.

Then he saw, stuck to the back of an envelope, a great, riotously colored post card. He bent down to read it, and cried out with love and misery at the snapshot of two small, savage figures hanging from the Eiffel Tower, each with a leg around a girder, leaning into space and waving at him. The message read:

> Just married.
> This is a great town.
> Joan and Merko

There was a hammering at the door. Rose clasped his hand. 'It's unlocked!' she called, and Swan burst into the room.

'Hal, boy! It's wonderful to have you back. Just in time! Come on, now. We've got everything at once to do this afternoon. First stop, the *Globe*, then the *Post*.'

'Are you sure it will be all right?' Rose inquired timidly. She made a sign to Swan, indicating that Hal was not very well. Swan didn't need to be told. It was obvious to him that Hingham was wobbly and would get worse if something wasn't done.

'Let's go,' he said. They went down in the elevator and Swan told them, with a wink: 'First stop, I want you to meet a friend of mine named Hennessy,' and he led them into the bar.

The brandy made Hal gasp. Soon he felt stronger, and it seemed

183

to him that a golden column had been sent up his spine. 'You like my friend, hey?' laughed Swan. 'Have another? You, too?' he added to Rose. They shook their heads. 'All right, we'll be on our way, then.' His property, he saw, had become much more presentable. Now the deal was to rush him through before the effect wore off.

Meanwhile Rose hung on to Hal's hand. She was fascinated yet frightened by Swan and the world of success he represented. If anything went wrong with Hal as a result of Swan's dragging him around, it would be on her conscience forever. Yet the publicity and all the honors could be so right for Hal's future and their future together. She nodded when Swan said: 'All right, kids.' She took Hal's arm and they followed him to a taxi.

The afternoon passed in a delirium of publicity. Hal learned from a series of press releases thrust under his nose in various taxicabs that his system was based on modesty. Swan had instinctively divined something of the nature of Centralism. He had hit on the term 'self-effacement' to describe Hal's secret. According to one of his releases:

'When I'm with a prospect I try to efface myself,' Hingham declared. 'I try to remember that where his needs are concerned, I do not exist,' the sensational young underwriter went on.

This line remarkably suited Swan's property of the afternoon, who appeared almost totally effaced by his good fortune. But it didn't matter. As Swan calculated, those who interviewed Hal were already so impressed by his record (which Swan had distributed separately) that although he was dazed and drowsy, murmuring he hardly knew what answers, Hal made a fine impression everywhere.

Jack Swan skillfully threw it away: 'As you may well believe, Hal is beat. He'd appreciate a little forbearance, but here he is . . .'

Hal simply hung on. One face after another came before him. Hands were put in his and withdrawn. Some of these people had notebooks. Others put microphones to his lips, and there were cameras everywhere.

'Now, what is it, Mr Hingham, that you believe to be at the bottom of your overnight success?'

'Modesty.'

'Really. That's interesting. And how did you – '

'In the Bible,' he replied, as Swan had coached him.

'Well, that's *marvelous*.'

They asked him about his relations with his father: 'You used to resent him?'

'Yes, but I got on top of my feeling and now I am glad that he provided me with a challenge,' he said, as he had memorized it in the cab.

Rose followed along helplessly. She was both thrilled and dismayed by Swan's headlong charge through the city's newspaper offices, and the radio and television stations. He was incredibly different from the darkly inhibited bantam suitor who used to wait on Gladys and Heffernan. Here he was a demon, dragging Hal to the desks of city editors, bullying his way past receptionists, and finally, still holding Hal by the hand, he walked past frantic signals into a television program and actually pushed his property in front of the camera.

At this point she felt that it was time for her to intervene. Hal was moving more and more like a robot. She looked into his eyes, and they were lifeless. He seemed to see nothing and care for nothing, although, curiously, he became increasingly polite to all who spoke to him. 'Yes, Mr Swan,' he said, and 'Yes, dear,' when she asked if he was tired.

'Can't we stop now? Remember, Hal has just come from a sickbed,' she appealed to Swan.

They were in the elevator, coming down from a television studio. 'Maybe you're right,' Swan agreed. He was smiling and breathing heavily. He stood with his hand slipped inside his jacket, and looked very much the leader. 'Yes,' he said, 'that ought to be enough for today. Don't forget, though, tonight Hal sleeps at your place.'

He sent them home in a cab. As Hal got in, he took Rose aside. 'You're going to the game tomorrow. That's fine. We'll all be able to keep an eye on each other. The problem is to keep everything on an even keel until Monday afternoon. Just don't tell him about the speech. Okay?'

Swan shook hands with Rose. 'By the way, if I come up, it won't be to see your roommate. I guess you know I'm through with her,' he said proudly.

35

Masks Off

Hal sat in the Bay State U. rooting-section with Rose and Gladys. They had seats near the bench, giving them a close view of Johnny Heffernan powering up and down the sideline with flailing elbows, preparing for the job he was going to do on the Norway Tech line. Also, near the bench, down among the players, was Jack Swan. He sat behind his typewriter at a long table with two college-boy assistants. His task was to provide the press with on-the-spot comment and color from the Bay State U. side. Now and then he spoke into a field telephone connecting him with the press box, but mostly he kept his eye on the Hingham party. He waved at Rose when the others weren't looking.

Three boys and three girls with megaphones turned cartwheels on the green, and Hal joined in a long cheer for Bay State U.

'Hal, look. Gladys has her name in the paper,' said Rose, handing him the sports page. He read the column:

COPP ON THE BEAT
BY EARL COPP

At Exeter Field, highly touted Bay State U. plays host to Norway Tech. This is supposed to be BSU's year, and on paper they are at least three touchdowns better than Skip Gautreau's Green Mountaineers. The huge BSU forward wall led by 240-pound Johnny 'Slam' Heffernan figures to spend the afternoon in Norway's backfield and mess up Skip's fast but fragile ball carriers before they can get started.

Incidentally, the Slammer threw a monster banquet for his mates last Tuesday to celebrate his engagement to beauteous Gladys Swaim, a nurse at Hartsdale Hospital. This kind of high-jinks is one reason why a few of the more cautious experts are wary of BSU. The question has been asked whether love and late hours are a suitable prelude to a contest with the mysterious Vermonters.

SURPRISED HARVARD
You can't afford to trifle with a Gautreau-coached outfit. The teams Skip

brings down here are usually small, but they can be tough and nasty – as surprised Harvard found out three years ago. Of course, Harvard isn't in the same class with BSU. Furthermore, Coach Ed Notsik claims that the midnight frolic for Heffernan and his bride-to-be was just the spate of relaxation his team needed.

The tea leaves tell us he is right. The pick here is BSU by 20–0. The forecast is for a middling-warm sunny day. This may take some of the starch out of Heffernan & Co, but it won't do the northerners any good either. Athletic Director Ed Maxwell expects a crowd of 20,000 or more for the season opener.

Gladys didn't appear to be moved by the story one way or another. She sat hunched over, brooding on the field. With a flowing maroon bandanna around her head and shoulders, she resembled a shawled peasant girl, bowed with labor. She chewed her gum like a cud. Only when Heffernan led the BSU team out on the field did she sit up and become a bit animated.

Hal shouted and groaned with the others to see what was going on out on the football field. It was unbelievable. Poor Ed Notsik was clawing the 'B' off his sweater and weeping. He was going to hear from the alumni.

'Rah!' Hal said feebly, along with Rose and Gladys and the rooters around him. There was little to cheer about. The BSU banners had fallen off everybody's knees. Norway was driving again. Skinny Villon sneaked through for seven. Poquelin plowed over left tackle for sixteen. Then Poquelin lateraled to Le Duc, who went all the way.

'Oh, how awful!' screamed Rose.

Poquelin kicked the point.

'Norway Tech is now FORTY-SIX' said the public-address announcer. 'Bay State. . .'

'NOTHING!' roared the Norway stands.

Everybody was drunk over there, and they had a right to be. Gladys sat with her chin on her fists. The tears of fury were gone, and she regarded the field with weariness and contempt. Her great shoulders quivered. Rose leaped up with every play, waving her banner no matter who had the ball. Out of the corner of her eye she watched Hal anxiously, and she listened to his exhausted shouts, longing to know what he was thinking.

He was thinking: 'It's the end, this is the end.'

187

The Team of Destiny lost its mask early. The visitors from Vermont ran like crazed billygoats through the hapless monsters. They sprang on Johnny Heffernan with knees and cleats. His formidable nose guard was elbowed off during the third play of the game. They ran around him and through him and over him. They laid him out like a corpse before his bride-to-be, and ran over his great shape as rodents do in an animated cartoon. Norway Tech thumbed its nose at everything Bay State University stood for. In the third quarter, with the whipped and panting monsters behind 27–0, one of Tech's watch-charm guards flung himself sideways and sickened Heffernan with a terrible belt in the gut. Amid absolute silence he was carried off the field.

'Stop him!' Rose begged, as Le Duc drove for the touchdown, and then turned in embarrassment to see Hal's reaction. She needn't have feared his opinion of her. He had no opinion. Life was a gray irrelevance. He saw through to the bones of people, not only through the flesh, but through the flesh of their thought to the skeletal motive. He found no motives. He found no reasons for what they did. They only moved. Rose's fingers and thumb clutching his arm felt like five little bones. Her prettified cries in response to the action on the field were for him caws for the tumblings of helmeted eyesockets, joints, and tendons. The program-vendors were selling painted woodpulp, and the scoreboard flashed numbers having nothing to do with the pile of bones on the chalk lines.

He had to move, and said: 'I've got to go to the bathroom.'

Under the stands, surrounded by steaming urinals, cigar smoke, and behatted men with scorecards, he forgot the game. He walked out, toward the streetcar line. Behind him, at intervals, he heard the roars from the stadium. She must be getting nervous about him now.

She had been nervous, and so was Jack Swan. They both made immediate decisions to follow him under the stands. As he saw Rose go out, Swan paused. Gladys was sitting alone, and he couldn't resist the temptation to go up to her.

'Congratulations, doll,' he said. 'Not every girl has her engagement announced in the sports pages.'

She looked at him without speaking, without interest.

'The bridegroom had his troubles today,' he said, but he was unable to get a rise out of her. In victory or defeat, she ignored him. He had an impulse to court disaster, to goad her to smash him or tongue-lash him in front of all these people, but the thrill was gone. She had already sunk into her approaching motherhood. Then he saw that Hingham hadn't come back, and headed for the exit.

Rose caught up with Hal at the streetcar stop. 'Hal,' she said, 'where are you going?'

He turned without surprise, as if he had expected the world to follow him, and had his answer ready.

'I'm going away,' he said.

'Why, dear? Where do you want to go?'

'To Dr Modesto. Where people won't notice me.'

Rose had no idea what he was talking about. She realized at this moment that Hal was virtually a stranger to her, and always had been. He was in some kind of torment beyond her understanding. His thin, pathetically agreeable face was averted from her. It was the face of a sensitive but mediocre boy of whom civilization had demanded too much, and he was through – through with it.

'Everybody please let me alone,' he said.

'Including me, Hal? You want *me* to leave you?' she cried.

'Yes, I do. I'm not good enough for everybody. I haven't the right. I can't ask everybody to share my life. I'm not worthy, and I broke the law. Forgive me,' he said, making for the turnstile. A trolley was coming.

'Hal, think of me. Not everybody. I love you! I'll work, and you won't have to sell any more insurance. Hal . . .'

He boarded the trolley and waved from the window, not to her but to everybody in the station. His lips formed the words: 'Forgive me!' and the car rolled around the corner.

'Oh, God, is it my fault?' Rose wept at the turnstile.

She was grasped violently by the elbow. 'What happened? Where is he?' demanded Jack Swan. 'I told you not to let him out of sight.'

'No, as I said, I wouldn't have the slightest idea where Mr Hingham might be,' the desk clerk repeated.

'But it's two in the morning,' said the ulcerated man before him. He waved the packet he was carrying, as though the sight of it would have to improve the clerk's memory. 'I'm his public-relations counsel. He – does he usually stay out this late?'

'I wouldn't know, sir,' replied the clerk, sorting a pile of slips.

'Look. This is – he's got to – '

'I believe you mentioned before that Mr Hingham must deliver a speech. But, you see, I don't know where he is.'

'I've been here since seven. There's no justice in this,' Swan whimpered.

He plucked a ten-dollar bill from his wallet, and placed it on the desk in front of the clerk, who looked sympathetically at the money.

The phone made a snickering sound, and the clerk answered it in the back office. It was some time before he came out.

'That wasn't – '

'No, sir. But, I tell you – why don't you take a nap and I'll wake you the moment he comes in.'

Swan walked unsteadily to a sofa. He huddled there against a hard green pillow, staring at the ceiling.

He was wakened by a gentle tug on the shoulder. The desk clerk was bending over him. 'Mr Hingham has just gone up to his room,' he whispered. 'He's checking out!'

'Oh, no, he isn't!' Swan staggered up, bleary-eyed and disheveled. The clock across the deserted lobby said it was six in the morning. He picked up Sunday papers from the reception desk. 'Mr Hingham is staying here until tomorrow morning. In the afternoon he makes the speech. I'm going to be with him until he does. My name's Swan' he said, handing the clerk another ten. 'Hold his room, and put me in with him.'

On his way up in the elevator, it occurred to Swan that what he was doing was something like kidnapping, but it was a chance he would have to take. 'After all,' he thought philosophically, 'an agent can't steal his own property.'

36

At the Convention

In the anteroom off Convention Hall, Fred Purdy had a partial view of the stage and the acreage of tables on the main floor. The delegates were resuming their seats after lunch. Around the hall, banners hung from the balcony and wobbling signs and placards designated the gathering-places of the state and city delegations. The subdued tumult gradually grew louder as the hall filled up. From time to time delegates were summoned over the loudspeaker. It was almost two o'clock, when the afternoon session would begin. Hingham was to speak at three.

There were heavy circles under Fred Purdy's eyes. He had slept poorly after receiving Swan's first phone call Sunday afternoon. It was not that Swan had bad news: 'I'm with him now, Fred. He's asleep. We've been over the speech, and we'll go through the rest of it tonight. Don't worry. He's co-operating, and I'm sticking with him until we meet you at the hall.' Again in the morning, this morning, Swan phoned to say that the situation was under control. Hingham was stronger, and eating, and seemed reconciled to making the speech. They had practiced reading again, and it had gone well. Swan sounded hysterically triumphant. He called attention to the 'forest fire' of publicity he had created for his property in the Sunday and Monday papers.

Purdy had gone past the point of worrying about his responsibility for the Hingham affair. A deeper worry left him slumped in the anteroom. For the first time in his life, he felt old and scared. During the past few days he had felt like a misfit and had lost his feeling of superiority to life. Somewhere, he had slipped. He had laughed at Swan and patronized him. Yet this half-educated little public-relations man had swept him out of his depth, and he was afraid. Swan was a new kind of operator, with a breath-taking contempt for people that made his own old-hat cynicism seem like that of a fuddy-duddy.

Bells began to clang around the hall. His program told him that Arthur from the home office was to speak; then Collins, also from New York; then Hingham, and the acting mayor. Purdy sat upright, in surprise. He thought he saw Hingham in the New Hampshire delegation – someone, anyway, walking around like a lost soul with his hat on at that peculiar angle. But then another delegate removed the chap's hat and eased him to a seat. Purdy went to the door and made sure that it was somebody else – a fellow apparently shaken by an extra martini at lunch.

With the rapping of the gavel, the speeches began. Purdy, from his vantage point behind the stage, had a rear view of the speaker. The home-office man told a mild joke, and the rows of empty faces laughed. 'How I envy them – they believe in it,' Purdy said to himself. They were earnest dolts, but they really believed in home and mother, in protecting their loved ones, in the rightness of all these foolish props that held up the life-insurance business. If he had felt any such faith in anything, he wouldn't have approved the exploitation of poor Hingham.

Time was going by, but he didn't give a damn. He refused to look at his watch. 'Poor Hingham, if I had only fired you,' he mused.

The home-office man sat down to the flapping of many hands, and Collins was introduced. As he got under way, Hingham came into the anteroom, followed by Swan, who wore an expression of unendurable satisfaction. Turning his back on the public-relations man, Purdy went to Hal and asked: 'How are you, boy?'

'I'm fine, Mr Purdy,' said Hal. He did feel fine, because all he had to do was make one very short speech, and he would be free to do as he liked. He would be able to go away, anywhere, if he wanted to, Jack Swan said. Jack Swan had written a wonderful speech for him. It was just right, because it would please everybody. That was all he had ever wanted to do – please everybody. Then they wouldn't blame him for what he had done that day in Bradford. If he read the speech *exactly* as it was written, Jack Swan promised, they would forgive him everything. Dr Modesto would be pleased; he would forgive him too. Jack Swan knew. There was not even any need to understand the words he was speaking. No, no, it was the material that counted. Hal Hingham was as good as his material.

'Sit down, Hal.'

'Thank you, Mr Purdy.'

'See what I mean, Fred? Am I right?'

Jack Swan was a fine man. He understood Centralism. He had spent the evening reading the Revelations, and he was going to book Dr Modesto on a lecture tour. This would be another reason why Dr Modesto would forgive him.

'How are you feeling, Hal? Want to go to the bathroom or anything?'

'No, thank you,' he said.

'Look at the press section, Fred. It's filled.'

After today, no one would ever possibly laugh at him, because they wouldn't see him. They never saw into a man who could please everybody, and they never, never laughed at him. He heard clapping, and Mr Purdy and Mr Swan each took him by the arm to the edge of a great lighted stage. He saw the backs of the heads of many older gentlemen, one of whom was bowing and sitting down. Another gentleman got up, and smilingly looked over his shoulder. 'He's looking at me,' Hal thought. This distinguished man spoke his name.

Mr Purdy and Jack Swan were talking into his ears at the same time, but he couldn't hear them because of the clapping. Then Jack Swan put the speech in his hands, and pushed him. He crossed the boards in the blazing light in front of all the people he was to please, so that he would be forgiven, and the gentleman conducted him to a semicircle of microphones.

It was terribly quiet, and he was all alone, as he had once dreamed, on Judgment Day. He looked down, as Jack Swan had instructed him, and read:

'My dear friends and fellow underwriters, you have honored me in such a way as I could never have dreamed a few short months ago when I walked into the office of Fred Purdy, and asked for his advice and help.

'I assure you that none of you would have blamed Mr Purdy for throwing up his hands and giving up on the spot. I was, you might say, a very poor risk.'

He started walking up and down before the microphones, with his suit flapping about his thin body. He held the speech close to his breast, like a book. He read from it fervently. He resembled a wrecked evangelist rising out of his own ruin through the power of the text in his hands, although he didn't comprehend a word of it.

'As one of the fellows at Commonwealth put it at that time: "Anyone who tries to teach Hingham anything deserves a medal for gallantry above and beyond the call of duty." But then . . .'

He paused, terrified by the roaring sound in front of him. He saw hundreds of faces laughing at him. Jack Swan had promised they wouldn't, but they were. They laughed because he hadn't been able to please them. They were telling him that he would never be forgiven for being Hal Hingham. He stepped back from the microphones, and Jack Swan's speech dropped from his hand. He understood now. All these people had come from Bradford. They were trying to trap him. He had sold them all policies, but to each one he had been a different person. Now they laughed: 'Please us all!' But he couldn't – not while they were all together. That was the trap. The only way for him to escape now was to stand up to them, let it be in high agony, and say: 'I am myself, as God made me, and this is the best I can do!'

But he had given himself away. He wasn't anybody.

The delegates saw him approach the microphones again. He peered among them with his great foolish eyes, looking for someone. Those on the west side of the hall, near the stage, were able to obtain Hingham's attention. The gentlemen on the stage exchanged whispers, and one tiptoed forward to pick up the discarded speech and hand it to the speaker. Before he could do so, Hingham leaned into the microphones and, without warning, brought them up out of their seats with a despairing shout: 'Merko!'

A trembling silence followed. Many of the delegates sat down shakily, and reached for handkerchiefs to wipe their faces.

Hingham began speaking in a sing-song: 'He's not here. It's too late. Too late for Hal. I'm sorry. He tried to be somebody, but he isn't. That's all right. I'm sorry, Dr Modesto. I'm coming to see you, and you will forgive me because I tried. Do you know what killed me? Life insurance. I hate life insurance, because it is death if you don't want to sell it and they make you. I love you, Dr Modesto, and I am coming. I like the new Ford. Sorry, Al, your Chevvy is better. Meant to say, Jim, it's Nash. One at a time, but you're all here. Let me go, and I'll be nice. Please!'

He wandered from the microphones and begged the gentlemen on the speakers' platform: 'Let me go. Everybody has a right to their opinion, if they don't abuse it. I never meant any harm. Love dogs, but not the one that dug up your garden. You see?'

A rumbling started up in the hall. He felt it coming like an express train. The gentlemen on the platform were getting up and reaching for him. He ran. They couldn't catch him. He ran into a little room and saw his hat on the table, and grabbed it. He escaped between Mr Purdy and Mr Swan, who had collapsed on a table with their heads buried in their arms. He went out a door, and fell over some cobblestones, and raced down an alley. After a while he began skipping, like a boy out of school.

37

Ace Insurance Salesman Flees Convention Hall

BAY STATE REGISTER: NEWS OF THE WEEK

The annual convention of the Arcadia Life Insurance Company was thrown into an uproar at Convention Hall last Monday when one of its featured speakers, 28-year-old salesman Hal Hingham, who had broken all company sales records this past summer, abruptly broke off his address to the delegates and ran from the stage.

Arcadia publicist Jack A. Swan said he attempted to restrain Hingham, but the latter broke free and rushed out the back door. Police said Hingham had disappeared in the network of alleys behind the hall. A search of the area revealed no trace of the missing salesman.

Company officials expressed confidence Monday that Hingham would 'be at his desk at nine o'clock in the morning.' However, Frederick Purdy, director of Arcadia Life's Commonwealth branch, refused to comment on this prediction. Later Swan gave the press an authorized statement from Purdy saying that Hingham had only recently recovered from pneumonia and 'presumably suffered a relapse' at the convention hall.

Witnesses agreed that Hingham showed signs of not being himself throughout his brief address. Departing from his prepared speech, he denounced life insurance in general and the Arcadia company in particular. In veiled language, he accused the company of putting some kind of pressure on him. Delegates close to the stage said he ran smiling to the wings. 'It was a strange smile, as if there wasn't anything behind it,' said Arnold O'Brien of Rochester, NY. Another delegate, Frank Moses of Nashua, NH, said he had seen Hingham the night before in the company of Swan at the Circle Hotel, 'looking very badly.' This was denied by the public-relations man, who said he had spent the evening at home.

The story has received considerable attention in the press, partly because of the extensive pre-convention publicity given Hingham. He was pictured as a failure who had achieved extraordinary selling results within a few weeks through a technique of 'self-effacement.' He said he had found this technique in the Bible. He had appeared on a number of television and radio programs just before the convention.

When Hingham failed to turn up at the Arcadia Life office on Tuesday morning, police stepped up their investigation of the salesman's recent movements. Across the country there were an unusually large number of cases of mistaken identity. Hundreds of persons have reported seeing Hingham, but always it was someone who wore his hat in the same way, or with a similar walk, but not Hingham. A promising lead blew up when the 'stranger' who called for Hingham at his hotel before dawn on Sunday turned out to have been Jack Swan. Pressed by newsmen, he replied: 'I'm in enough trouble as it is. The whole thing went wrong, that's all. Can't you fellows give me a break?'

Reporters have been unable to question Purdy, Hingham's immediate superior. Purdy was said to have arranged for Hingham's appearance as a convention speaker. It was noted that the salesman's prepared address contained a tribute to the agency-director as the man who had 'inspired' him.

Purdy's refusal to see newsmen heightened the mystery aspects of The Hingham Story. On the second day, the press became openly suspicious that Arcadia was hiding something. The vanished salesman was assumed to be a victim of hidden pressures. In his 'Window on Boston,' George Stillman led off:

Monday afternoon you watched a man fall slowly to pieces. . . . It wasn't pretty. . . . In the beginning, there was a human being like yourself. You joined in the applause. . . . He started speaking, and suddenly you wondered: 'Is *this* the boy they're all talking about?' . . . It was a boy whose speech was rambling and hysterical and gradually tortured into some gibberish known only to himself . . . Here's one observer who wants to know what gives. . . . Where is Hal Hingham?

The gossip columnists have had inside stories. One said that Hingham had been placed in a private retreat by Arcadia. Another learned that he had recently been under a psychiatrist's care. A third reported that the salesman had an incurable disease.

On Wednesday, a chilly item appeared:

... Arcadia Life biggies in from New York to nail those responsible for Hingham fiasco ...

After three days had gone by, Hingham was still missing. Opinion crystallized into the general idea that the boy's breakdown and disappearance were due to Arcadia's exploitation of a sensitive nature. Clearly, a monumental public-relations blunder had taken place.

The column 'Nick Hendrix Says' was addressed to one of the principals:

Jack Swan. You're a little guy, not very tall. But full of big ideas. A press agent, that's you – until a few years ago you landed the Arcadia Life account, and overnight that turned you into a Public Relations Counsel.

So you were a Public Relations Counsel for a big insurance outfit. A big deal. The razzle-dazzle you used to employ for Gypsy Manic and her invisible shawls didn't go any more. No, this was a real respectable affair. You almost forgot you were a hustler.

You buttoned up your pin-stripe so that the yellow checkered vest wouldn't show. But it was there. It had to show sooner or later, even if the stunt you pulled sent a poor kid into his private oblivion.

You always had a great sensa humah, Swanee. I have a new laugh for you. The Public Relations Association held a meeting last night. They voted an inquiry into your campaign. And let me make a prediction, Swanee. When they expel you, not one voice will be raised in your defense. After tomorrow, Swanee, you'll have to go to work for a living.

More philosophically, Rex Lieber attributed Hingham's sufferings to the mounting pressures of the era, a country-wide loss of absolute values, and cynical company policy. 'A publicity man's dream becomes a nightmare,' he wrote, 'and the age of public relations claims another victim.'

The Hingham Story reached a plateau of interest on Friday. The Insurance Agents union accused Frederick Purdy of tyrannizing over Arcadia underwriters and driving Hingham to a nervous breakdown. A popular minister, the Reverend Peter Snowden of Hampton, assailed the company for its unscrupulous and un-Christian principles. Hingham's fiancée, Rose Thatcher, appeared on a television program and made an appeal to him to come home. Her message has not been answered.

The police have no clues to Hingham's whereabouts. He might be anywhere. Little more can be said about Hal Hingham until he is located or comes forward voluntarily to clear up the mystery of his strange flight.

38
Rewards and Punishments

Purdy watched Swan bow out of his office, but the satisfaction he had looked forward to for so many hours didn't come to him. 'He took it so well,' he meditated. 'That's why I didn't get any pleasure.' He felt a perverse admiration for Swan. The public-relations operator had never so much dignity as when he was fired. 'That's all right, Fred. No hard feelings.' It must have been this same jauntiness that carried him safely through the meeting of the Public Relations Association. He had been able to get off without suffering a vote of censure or even a reprimand. Swan accepted such ups and downs as part of an operator's career. 'I'm not so resilient,' Purdy said to himself.

He gazed out at the gloomy autumn afternoon. Great cold winds were whipping about the sky, and he thought: 'That's all we're afraid of – being out in the cold.' He had something to believe in at last – keeping warm. It occurred to him that he had just sent Swan out to that cold wind.

He laughed savagely at his somber mood, and asked himself since when guilt had entered his life. Swan had fouled Arcadia's name. The penalty was automatic. Purdy stared at his barren desk blotter. He couldn't get Swan's dignity out of his mind. The cashiered public-relations man had refrained from embarrassing him with the truth that they were equally guilty of sponsoring Hingham's appearance.

When his time came, he too would bow out like a sport, to keep the as-if going.

The door opened and a man walked in without knocking. Purdy recognized the narrow bald head and pointed jaw. Mr — from the home office.

'Mr —' he said, getting up.

'Blake.'

'Sure! I guess you and I've had a world's record for correspondence on that Hingham business. Wasn't that awful? You know, it's a shame. If you'd been here five minutes ago. I just informed Mr Swan, as per – '

'Fired him, eh?' the other said. He placed his hat on the rack in a certain way. 'Blind leading the blind, I'm sorry to say.'

'It hits first in the gut,' Purdy mused.

'Somebody's head, Mr Purdy – heads roll, you know, after a fiasco.'

'I'm – '

'I've come to relieve you.'

'I'm – ?'

'Oh no, not dismissed. The company feels you're much too good a salesman. We're only relieving you of your administrative duties.'

'You can't,' said Purdy. They couldn't deprive a man of his way of life for one isolated mistake. 'Back where I started from?' he asked. 'An ordinary salesman?'

'We have no ordinary salesmen,' said the man from New York.

Not to have this office any more. Stripped of his genial authority. It wasn't a game.

'How about you!' he flared up. 'You approved the Hingham publicity. I've got correspondence to prove . . . Just because you're in the home office!'

'On the contrary, I've been demoted to your position. Was that a washroom I saw in the hall?'

Purdy dwelt mutely on the gunmetal back of his replacement. He turned to the window. He saw dozens of salesmen struggling through the bone-chilling wind, and thought: 'It's cold, for a man my age.'

The little church was filled with football-players, as well as bridesmaids and flower girls, and a number of old people crying happily. The organ played 'Oh, Promise Me' and soon Gladys came down the aisle. Her voluminous wedding gown flowed across the aisle, and the husky bridegroom stumbled over it. He gave vent to a whispered imprecation, but then resumed his embarrassed grin as they made their way past the pews. As Gladys passed Rose, she smiled faintly, and then she was gone into the sunlit lawn with Johnny Heffernan, accompanied by an honor guard of his teammates.

Rose waited in her pew until the last wedding guest had left the church. Outside, she felt a tap on her shoulder. It was Jack Swan. He motioned in the direction of the bridal party. 'Touchdown,' he said.

She turned away from him.

'What's the matter? Are you angry with me?' he asked.

She stood up and walked slowly away from him, saying: 'I am absolutely contemptuous of you. Don't speak to me.'

'Contempt?' he replied, with an edge of excitement in his voice. He followed her. 'Why? How could I know what was going to happen to Hal? Please, don't turn your back. Rose!'

She continued walking slowly.

'Let me make it up to you. I can't stand your looking down on me. I want to see you,' he begged at her shoulder.

They were on the gravel path together. He was regarding her impudently, and at the same time with a sort of obsequiousness. 'You and I have a lot in commmon, Rose. If you can't like me, at least see me now and then.'

He reminded her of a mouse, nosing around. The way he eyed her, she felt her body like a trap.

'Can I call you, Rose?'

'All right,' she said.

39

Through the Curtain

The Cornhusker Limited rushed toward Omaha.

'Omaha in twenty minutes!' shouted the conductor in the club car, and got no reaction at all. The passengers had fixed their attention on a curtain of dust and rain developing to the south. They sipped their drinks and declined to look at him.

'What a bunch of deadheads,' the conductor said to himself. He had noticed the same kind of people in all the cars. A lot of guys with vacant eyes, and they wore their hats on a slant. For instance, the fellow in the last chair, looking out on the back of the train. His hands hung down in a peculiar way. He simply stared at the retreating landscape. The conductor left, shaking his head.

From the observation car Hal was watching tracks, telephone poles, bushes, the world, receding swiftly and endlessly. All the objects he discovered immediately became smaller and smaller and vanished. All things were vanishing in one great flight away from him. As life emptied out of him, only the tracks were the same.

'A nice fellow,' said a man in the club car.

'Yes, I talked with him. A student.'

'Hardware salesman,' corrected the other.

'Pardon me, I happened to talk with him, I said.'

'Well, so did I, my friend.'

The old lady sipped her ginger ale with a smile, knowing that the nice boy was going to Broad View to live with his father.

40

Occupational Therapy

'So long as you're a staff man, I'll be glad to show you around,' the director said. 'It's these free-lancers, so-called, that get my ass. The times I've rolled out the carpet for some guy with no connections at all. . . . I suppose you want to know about the Broad View System, and MacIlwain. What are you, Mr Files? A science writer?'

'No,' said the reporter. 'I write features – human-interest stuff. You see, I took my vacation in the East this year. I thought if I stopped on my way back to the coast I might pick up a few columns. There's a lot of curiosity about Broad View in our area – with all the movie people checking in here, you can imagine. You've got a lot of human interest here, Mr Denny. People would like to learn how the System works. I'm very anxious myself.'

'You must be,' said the director in an amused tone. 'To detour out of your way like this. What did you do? Take the branch line from Omaha?'

'Yes. I hope to get back in time to catch the west-bound tonight, if possible.'

The director heaved himself to his feet. He was an obese man, so much so that he was unable to stand erect. His abdomen jutted drum-tight from below his belt. His expression was one of savage merriment, with a suggestion of agony, as if a terrible thing was about to happen to him if he didn't empty his bladder soon. Yet he pushed the reporter past the men's-room door, saying: 'This way, Mr Files.'

In the corridor he went on: 'You're probably talking to the wrong man. I'm strictly a fund-raiser. You need somebody with a more romantic approach. Or one of the nut specialists. Oh, I'll take you around, but the man you ought to see is MacIlwain. You won't, though. He's off on another lecture tour. Now, there's a smart operator.'

The director bared his teeth, and at the same time his arm shot out toward a passing nurse, who gave a tiny scream and evaded him. Mr Denny chuckled at his visitor, whose nervous eyes had sought the wall until the nurse was gone.

'Yes, sir, you're talking to the wrong man. Of course, I can tell you how the MacIlwain System works – that's what draws the crowds, all the writers, ever since he cured that first movie actor. I mean, I can give you the dope, but probably not with the right note of worship in my voice. Now, don't get the wrong impression. I'm not knocking MacIlwain. Hell, he's the greatest – '

A slant-hatted young man stepped from behind a pillar and said: 'Pardon me, but which way is Dr Modesto's office?'

'*Office*? Downstairs and around the circle,' the director said, and continued: 'Remember, I'm only the fund-raiser. Between you and me, sometimes I get pretty sick of it.'

'I'd like to know more about the MacIlwain System. It doesn't seem to me that you take it very seriously,' the reporter said.

'Take it seriously! My boy, you're unjust to me. Quickly let me cross myself. I love MacIlwain and am pleased to be a humble foot soldier in his crusade for mental health. These lunatics get my ass, that's all. I can't help it. *I don't like nuts.*'

They approached a small staircase. Mr Denny labored up the steps; his grin was fiercer and merrier.

'Another thing. Do you think it's any pleasure to be living here surrounded by a community of nuts so far from the city? Why couldn't MacIlwain have located closer to civilization?'

'Excuse me, how do I get to Dr Modesto's office?' inquired the smiling young man.

Mr Denny frowned and looked at him, and said: 'Down two flights and around the circle.' Watching the fellow go, he muttered: 'I told him once before.'

'No, that was another one. That one was stocky, and this last man was tall and thin. It was the hats, I think,' the reporter said.

'The MacIlwain System,' proclaimed Denny with facetious grandeur. He moved his hands before the reporter's face in a vulgar imitation of the hypnotist's art. 'Treat your patients as if they were normal. Approximate the conditions of real life. Then let them live according to their images of themselves. Within reason, of course,' the director amended, bitterly imitating the tone of a fuddy-duddy scholar. 'Give them the tools of life. My God, you don't believe me! These nuts have stethoscopes and dictaphones.

They have guns. No, they aren't loaded, but how would you like to have these creeps go pow and bang at you, and not be able to deny that you're an enemy agent. You saw that postman who went by just now. He's not real. He only *wants* to be a postman, but under the MacIlwain System he's allowed to carry real letters. It gets ridiculous. We have a bank! An amnesiac embezzler is in charge. The craziest goat at Broad View runs the printing-press. That's our philosopher, Dr Modesto, the one these fellows have been asking to see. He actually placed an ad in a magazine without our knowing it. Now he gets answers. His fans write him letters! Get the idea? This is the MacIlwain System in action.'

'I like it. I like seeing how it works,' the reporter said.

'Well,' said the director with a sidelong glance at him, 'you're only here for a couple of hours. It looks fine from the outside – '

'But Dr MacIlwain obviously answers a big need. Isn't there a waiting list of people all over the country trying to get in here?'

'A waiting list!' said Denny. 'They don't wait. They just arrive and expect their poor little personalities to be taken care of. We have to shovel them out of here. In the last few months there's been more and more. Amnesia cases, MacIlwain says. The whole goddamned country is forgetting itself – '

'Will you tell me, please, where can I find Dr Modesto?'

'He was the same! The same one who asked before! There's something funny going on,' Denny said. 'Never mind, the hell with it. I want to show you something in this room here. I always get a laugh.'

They went on through a door into a roomful of wandering men in red bathrobes. As they crossed the threshold, Denny thrust his sweaty, fat-creased visage into the young reporter's face and, breathing clove scent on him, said with desperate levity: 'What I want to know is, who takes care of *my* personality? Who takes care of a slob?'

The reporter turned away from him. 'Look at these people! What's wrong with them?' he asked.

'Ha, ha. Here's the saddest bunch of all,' the director said. 'The ones who tried to set themselves above the rest, and couldn't make it, and their consciences are gradually tearing them apart. They wanted to be the big shots. You know, financiers, scientists, writers, all that . . .'

'What makes that poor man hide his head?' asked Files. 'Is he afraid?'

'It's always so. When strangers come, it scares him,' Denny said.

'And how about that other one who ducked behind the couch?'

'He thinks you've come to rob his bank,' said Denny, 'and he's left the vaults unlocked. I'll show you something now. Don't think it's cruel, because their memories are shot and two minutes from now they won't remember that I spoke to them.

'Hey, Mr Malcolm, how's that great novel coming?' Denny shouted.

The man covered his head and groaned.

'George! Hey, George Conrad, how's the international banker.'

And this man turned away in agony.

Denny stopped. 'There's something going on here.' He was staring beyond the banker and the novelist.

'Yes, yes, there they are,' whispered the reporter.

Two more smiling, slant-hatted strangers were approaching them from the other end of the ward.

Denny seized the reporter by the elbow and turned him around, and there were three gentle young men behind them.

And then they were surrounded, and five gentle *pardon me's* fell on their ears, and the same question came from the lips of all the young men:

'Where can I find Dr Modesto?'

Denny lowered his head and walked away, grunting and straining for speed, followed by six young men.

He went down in an elevator full of strangers – all smiling, vacuous young men.

In the corridor dozens of them were emerging from behind pillars.

He heard shouts that came closer. There was the sound of trampling. Nurses and ward boys were running through the corridors crying out:

'Mr Denny!'

'Mr Denny!'

'Mr Denny!'

The young men in slanted hats were piling up in front of Modesto's cell. Dozens more, just alike, were joining them every minute. The cell bars rattled like hail. Through the crowd Denny caught a glimpse of the flashing eyes, the beard, and Dr Modesto's thunderous voice commanding him: 'Let my sons in! Let my sons in!'